MW01228338

GRANDFATHERS' CAVE

Kirby Records

Mountain Man Press
North Powder, Oregon

Kirby Records / Mountain Man Press
P.O. Box 107
North Powder, Oregon 97867
www.MountainManPress.com

Publisher's Note: This is a work of fiction. Names, characters, places, and incidents are a product of the author's imagination. Locales and public names are sometimes used for atmospheric purposes. Any resemblance to actual people, living or dead, or to businesses, companies, events, institutions, or locales is completely coincidental.

Book Layout ©2013 BookDesignTemplates.com
Edited by Susan Parrish

Ordering Information:
Quantity sales. Special discounts are available on quantity purchases by corporations, associations, and others. For details, contact the "Special Sales Department" at the address above.

Grandfathers' Cave / Kirby Records. -- 1st ed.
ISBN 9781495938160

*Dedicated to Norman and Holly Records
The most supportive parents anyone could hope for.*

Special thanks to my good friends, Bradley and Heather Phillips.

Disclaimer

Although this book is a fiction story, many of the survival skills depicted are real and the author has practiced them on outings into the forests of Eastern Oregon. The author wishes to encourage trying some of these skills under parental supervision. There are a few considerations.

The traps discussed can be made, but are illegal in most cases. They can cause serious damage to the practitioner if not careful. They will cause damage or death to small household pets as well as wild creatures, if left unattended. Better to make it a live trap for practice by using a box rather than a large stone.

Flint knapping is breaking sharp rock, some very much like glass. The shards can cause severe lacerations even to experienced knappers. Always take precautions to protect yourself and those around you when knapping.

Brain tanning exposes the practitioner to any diseases the animal might have. Brains and animal fat spoil quickly and cause a disagreeable stench as well as picking up harmful bacteria. Always protect yourself from exposure when tanning hides.

Building a fire can be dangerous especially when handling dry wood or grass that has been lit. Melted pitch will stick to and severely burn if it gets on your skin. Fire can get away from you if there is dry fuel nearby to catch it. Please protect yourself and the surrounding area when practicing fire skills.

It is always wise to have a partner when practicing primitive skills in case of an accident. If you try any of the skills depicted in this book, please do so with an adult partner.

Always enter the woods prepared to spend the night. Carry a lighter even if you intend to start your fire with friction. Carry food even if you intend to live off the land. Carry warm layers of clothing even if you intend to use survival shelter. Practice to gain the knowledge, but do not put yourself in harm's way while practicing.

Please visit a primitive skills gathering to learn more. There is a list of gatherings known to the author in the appendices. A list of recommended reading and glossary of primitive skills terms are also provided.

List of Illustrations

CHAPTER ONE

Alone

It was dark. There were no sounds other than those of the resident crickets chirping, water dripping, and a gentle breeze as it scraped itself across stone. It was peaceful, unlike the screams he had heard earlier. Screams of pain, screams of fear, screams of hate.

He had remained in his hiding place where he had been put, burrowing deep back under the rock shelf, as deep as he could squish. He was small, a surviving advantage under the circumstances. He had been given a container of dried meat that was packed for a long journey, to keep safe with him. He was wrapped in a fur robe more to quiet any sound he might make than to keep him warm, although it had done both. Water was near as it always had been. The trickling water from underground seepage gave him a familiar sound to concentrate on.

After the screaming had stopped, there were other sounds: sounds of scuffling coming from the cave floor in front of the rock shelf; rummaging sounds, grunting sounds, gathering sounds. He feared they were looking for him. Smaller rocks and sticks had been placed in front of the shelf as if they were part of the natural lay of the ground. This helped conceal his position. Care had been taken to protect him, although no one could have foreseen the outcome this time.

Once he had burrowed as deep as he could get, he had been quiet, ever so careful not to move an arm or a leg or to cry out. Ever since he was an infant, he had been taught that it was better to be silent, to listen, and to know what was around him, than to make sounds and lose track of potential dangers. To attract attention to oneself could put both him and those he cared about in danger.

Then there was silence, silence that lasted for a very long time. There also was the stench of blood in the cave. Not the smell of fresh meat that was familiar but a more wicked smell. He was scared. Sleep took him, or maybe he had passed out from the fear. Either way, it had been a relief.

He awoke to different sounds. This time he recognized the sounds of the four-legged hunters. He had always been told that they would eat him just as they did the smaller four-legged gatherers of the forest. His fear was renewed. One of the hunters knew he was there. It was sniffing at the rock edge and scraping with its paws. The whining it emitted had a sense of urgency to it. The other hunters ignored this one. There was plenty to eat left just outside the cave. Once again, sleep took him.

When he awoke, light seeped in from the edge of the rock shelf. He could see where a rock or two had been moved by the prying nose of a wolf and the scratch marks where its claws had scraped the rock about an arm's length from where he lay. He was thirsty. The water that trickled through the cave wasn't far, but he would have to expose himself a bit to get to where his lips could reach it. What if the wolves were still in the cave? What if the two-legged enemies were still close? No, if the two-legged were there, they would have fought the four-legged. If the sharp toothed hunters were still close, they would be making their sounds and sniffing at his hiding place.

He decided to risk it. His muscles ached as he crawled to the damp channel in the rock where the water was running. They ached from dehydration, but mostly from the tenseness of being scared for so long. The water tasted good at first. He drank deep but the water didn't sit well, and he threw it back up. It had been too much, too quickly. He had no idea how long he had been hidden. He hadn't eaten, he was not hungry. He sipped a little more water, instinctively knowing he must. A pit in his stomach grew from what he knew was true, but refused to think about. He was alone. Nobody was coming back for him. He scrunched back into this hiding place and slept again.

He was awakened by a distant sound of the four-legged hunters fighting. The night was very dark, but he could tell the fight was outside the cave down the slope near the base of the hill. Down the steep embankment on the rocks below, the boy heard a larger predator dragging off what he could of the spoils of war while the hunters barked and nipped at him. The boy listened as the fight moved out into the forest and then was gone over the next rise where sound was muffled. He was so tired from the emotional strain of fear that he slept again.

It was light out when he next awoke. He lay quietly and listened, but no sounds of fighting could be heard. Instead, he heard birds— lots of them—laughing and cackling. He knew that the birds would not be laughing, but screaming warnings, if the hunters were still close. He crawled out cautiously and looked around the cave. Though he had lived here for most of the previous winter, the cave looked strange to him now. It was taller than a man's head at the cave entrance but just barely. Its arched ceiling stayed about that same height for quite a ways until the floor rose up to nearly meet it. The floor was mostly solid rock near the front of the cave. An underground water source emerged from under a rock shelf to the rear, south side of the cave. The water trickled through a channel in the rock to the northern front of the cave where it tumbled down to join a larger stream and then on to the river. The channel had been carved by the water itself through gentle caressing of the solid rock through time immemorial. It created small, slow-moving pools and narrow, fast-moving rivulets and had sustained life in the cave for as long as its water had moved across that stone.

At the rear of the cave, just past the first rise in the floor, the stone ended. Dirt that had filled the cavern crevasses, blown in by wind or sifting down through minute cracks in the stone above the cave rose up, narrowing any passage to disguise a small room beyond

this crawlspace. This room contained the remnants of the grandfathers: fragile bits of a braded basket, tiny pieces of bone and stone
tools, flat rocks stacked with a purpose. The ancestors had lived here
so many years ago that nobody remembered the people or what they
were like. So long ago that dirt had buried much of what they had left
behind. But what they had built still remained.

His hiding spot was a heavy rock shelf that protruded from the
southern side of the cave. It was thick rock and low to the ground. It
had been used as a seat by the woman as well as the men. But the
boy was still small enough to crawl underneath, so it became his hiding place.

After another drink of water, he suddenly was aware of how
hungry he was. He had no idea how many days had passed since he
had been hidden away. He ate a little of the dried meat mixed with
berries from the rawhide box that was hidden with him. The box was
made of the skin of the large four-legged grass eaters that had been
killed by the two men. The deer skin had been worked by the woman
to remove the hair and meat.

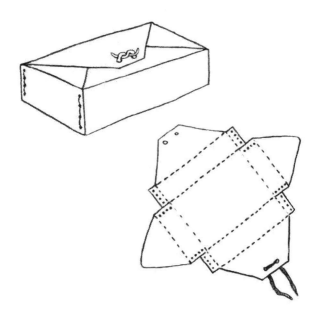

It had been stretched thin, cut, and folded while it dried. She had made a tough rodent-resistant container to hold dried meat or other precious items. It would last many years as long as it was kept dry.

He closed the flaps tightly, and tied them shut with the attached rawhide straps. He left it wrapped in the robe he had been sleeping in. The robe was made of the skins of four-legged hunters. It was soft and fluffy on one side but had the long black, white, and brown hairs of wolves on the other side. It had kept him and the woman warm at night when they slept. By himself he could fold it over and crawl in between the layers, which kept his feet warm. He tucked the whole bundle back under the rock shelf in case he had to hide in a hurry.

He walked toward the mouth of the cave. The crescent of stone that had held fire for cooking and warmth was scattered along with all the ashes. Enemy footprints criss-crossed the cave floor where they had kicked out the ashes, then searched the cave for any tools or food of value.

There were footprints of the animals that had moved in to scavenge after the enemies had left. Fire was not a friendly smell to the four-legged of the forest, so they had walked around the fire coals, but had still blackened their pads in the cold soot spread around the cave floor. The boy crept outside the mouth of the cave, keeping close to one edge and low to the ground so that anything watching from a distance would not easily see him. The bright sun warmed him and felt good. He squinted and listened for any signs of danger. It had been a long winter of little food and long walks in the snow.

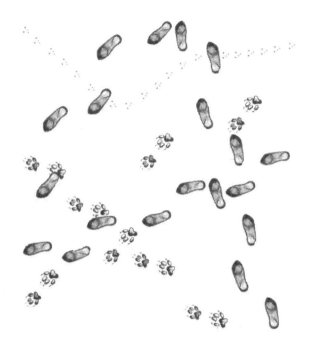

The cave faced southeast. From his vantage point, he saw the river in the bottom of the draw below him make its long, deepening curve into the sunrise. Snow lined the shadowed edge of trees and rocks, but on a few patches of ground, the dried grass of last fall showed through. The time of green grass was nearly here. He had looked forward to adding the various flavors of the different leaves to his diet again. The woman had known all the best ones to pick. He did not but had been with her enough times on her gathering forages to know one or two plants that he especially liked.

There were the bare trees that lined the river in places. There was the short cliff immediately below him and the rock rubble spreading out below the cliff down nearly to the valley floor. The sun was just up off the distant mountains and was trying to hide behind a dark but too-small cloud. The short-lived effect was brilliantly yellow rays of light emanating from the darkened cloud, lighting separate points in the pine forest that rose off the river into the eastern foothills. There were grey spots in the draws that held cottonwood or aspen trees. The trees were still bare and grey now, but had been brilliantly yellow in the fall. He had only been in this cave since midwinter, but he had lived in this type of forest all his life.

He looked down the short cliff to where the birds were making a racket. He didn't like what he saw. Now it was just a bloody stain, but the broken spear told him the truth of the matter. It was the spear of the older man of the cave. The spear was broken off about halfway down from the fire-hardened tip. The other end lay across several large boulders. The birds had been cleaning up the bits left by the predators that he had heard in the dark.

The boy worked his way down the path to the side of the embankment. He scattered the birds as he got closer, picked up the spear tip, and turned away. He had retrieved what he wanted and left quickly. He did not want to think about what had happened there.

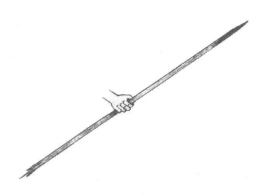

On the way back up to the cave, he stopped to dig out the root of a plant he knew was safe to eat. As he bent over, he spotted a glint under a nearby bush and picked up the shiny object. It was part of a stone spear tip. Made of a black stone that reflected the sun and broke easily, it was sharp on all edges. It had probably broken in the fight. The diagonal break had removed what had been the stem hafted into the wood of the spear shaft, but there was still a useful knife in the remaining blade. He carefully held it so as not to cut himself. He had seen blades like this before but had never been allowed to own one.

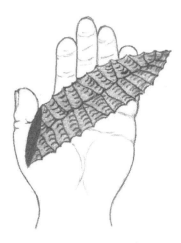

He scurried back up the trail. Inside the cave he placed his two findings on the rock shelf and began looking around the cave for anything else that might be of use. Not much was left, just the things that had been too heavy to carry, such as the old grinding stone used by the grandmothers a long time ago. The woman would have used it too, but they had not lived here during the time of seed gathering. He moved the fire rocks back into place. He piled the scattered wood next to it as it had been before. He did not know how to make fire, but he often had gathered firewood with the woman so that when the men had returned from the hunt, everything would be ready to begin cooking.

Down in a crack in a rock something caught his eye. It was a short piece of wood with cordage string wound upon it. The enemies must have missed it. This represented a lot of work by the woman, who had carefully cut the plants with jagged leaves that sting your skin and make it itch.

She had cooked the leaves to eat, but dried the stalk. She had crushed the outer layers, pulled out the long fibers, and twisted them into the string he was looking at now, rolling it up on the stick for later use. She had carried her string stick with her all the time. She had brought it in the leather box which now held dried meat, when she and the boy had run in the night. That was before they had met the men.

He suddenly missed the woman. He had spent all his short life close to her. He felt tears well up in his eyes. He sat down and cried silently. The day passed quickly in his mind. He was waiting, but he was not sure what he was waiting for.

The chill came on suddenly. Light was fading again. The boy ate another bit of food from the bag, drank from the cave water, crawled into the furs, and wriggled his way back under the rock shelf. This time, he took the short spear he had found with him. It was heavy for him, but he could handle the length. He felt better with the spear near.

"Boy" is all they had called him. A person had to earn a name. He had just begun going out with the men who would have found his name for him. Their names were good names.

"Two Bears" was the older man. He had earned his name when hunting a bear. He had speared one bear when another had appeared. He had to remove his spear earlier than he had wanted to from the first bear to stop the second bear from mauling his friend. He saved his friend and managed to kill both bears although he had also acquired several new scars in the process. Two Bears had wrinkles in his skin, especially around his eyes when he told stories to the boy and around his mouth when he laughed. His hair was grey with black streaks and hung down to the middle of his back when loose. He liked to keep it in two braids which he tied up in small ribbons of buckskin colored with the juice of red berries. The ribbons had been a gift from a woman, but he didn't talk much about her.

"Talking Elk" was the second and younger man. He was named when he learned to imitate the sounds of the larger red deer of the forest. Using his voice, he could lure the larger deer in close to other hunters. His hair was all black and kept in the two braids. He looked like Two Bears in the face, but he was taller and younger. He didn't talk to the boy as much, but he was a hard worker and a good hunter. He had gone out with the crude spears they had made, and he managed to keep them all fed this past winter.

Even the woman had a good name: "Fire Woman." Talking Elk said it was because she had so much fire inside that a man could be burned by her tongue. She had told Boy that she had won that name as a young girl when she had started a fire in the rain quicker than two boys her age. The boys were not really pleased, but an old man of her clan saw her expertise and had named her in front of the whole tribe. Fire Woman was taller than the boy, but not as tall as Two Bears. Her black hair fell below her waist when it was loose. She wore her hair in two braids, but decorated differently than the men. She was younger than Talking Elk but old enough to be his woman. He had treated her kindly. She had become his woman this past fall when he had protected her and Boy from the enemies who had come looking for them. She had made him promise he would train Boy in all the skills a hunter should know--skills that Boy would have learned at a younger age had he grown up in his own tribe. Two Bears thought it might be a good thing for Talking Elk to take a woman, and he had promised to help with Boy too.

Fire Woman was proud of her name and had kept the name even in the tribe that taken her captive. This had been the only people Boy could remember, the tribe they had run from in the night.

Boy figured he would never have a name now. The thought saddened him. Fire Woman had figured he was close to being ten winters old with the passing of this last winter, although she was not sure. When they met, he had been a small boy who still needed care.

He also had been a captive and did not speak the people's language when he was brought to her. The tribe had not allowed him to play or learn with the other boys. He had been taught to do the unwanted work for the captors. They had called him names, spat on him, and told him he was worthless.

The men they had met when they were running—Two Bears and Talking Elk—had been different. Mostly they had ignored the boy, but when they did include him, they had treated him with respect. They regarded him as the responsibility of the woman, but also as part of their newly formed group. As such, his work was valued as much as their own and he would have to do whatever he could to help them all. He had gathered firewood and kept the fire going while the others hunted or cooked or made new tools. Boy knew his job well, and the men had told the woman that he was a good worker. They had said this when he was close enough to hear. Boy never had felt valued like that before in his life. It was a good feeling. The men had promised Fire Woman they would begin taking the boy with them on the spring hunts once game was plentiful. Two Bears had taught him some things that could be taught in a winter cave with no preparation.

When they had run the second time, they all had to make what tools they could to replace those that had been left to the enemies. The enemies accused the men of taking their servants. Young warriors, who were quick to seek vengeance, kept on their trail until winter had blown in and sent them back to their people. The men had lost their weapons and tools in the running battle while they had protected Fire Woman and the boy. When a great snow came, it cut off the warriors' advance, and the two men, Fire Woman, and Boy had kept on moving.

They had no choice but to find shelter. Two Bears knew about a cave where the grandfathers had lived. He had been there once, but it had been hard to find in the driving blizzard. Once they reached the cave, they found dry firewood piled high inside. It was all small sticks. Two bears had pointed out where a family of small furry rats had built their lodge in that way. They had burned the wood for warmth until they could go collect more.

In the glow of their first fire in the cave, Two Bears had pointed out the paintings on the cave walls. He had only been here briefly a long time ago and had not lingered. This time he studied the drawings. Some were of people in strange dress and some were of animals. Two Bears recognized most of the animals, but some he was not familiar with. The drawings had been there for so long that no-body remembered the people who had painted them.

When the storm ended and the sun came out, their attention turned to food. Two Bears told Boy to consider the things they needed first to live. First was always water. Water is what made their body work right. Without water, you would only live for a few days. They had snow and the cave had a stream through it, so they did not need to spend time on that now. Next was shelter, which was im-portant to keep them from getting too cold. If they got too cold, they would not think right and could make bad decisions that could get them into trouble or cause them to freeze to death. Now they had the cave to stay dry and out of the wind. They also had their robes to wrap up in, and Fire Woman had made fire, which was even better. Next, they needed food. They could live for days or weeks without food but would get weaker and weaker. Food was now what they needed to find.

With the first break of the storm, Talking Elk went out looking for tracks and checking for signs of the enemy. Two Bears went out gathering materials to make hunting weapons. The men made spears of strong, straight wood. They sharpened the points while sitting around the cave fire and hardened the tips in the fire. Talking Elk brought in a deer with his spear. He was a great hunter and took very seriously his responsibility to provide food. It was a heavy snow win-ter and animals were difficult to find, but even with limited tools, he brought in enough meat to keep them alive. They were hungry all the time, but Fire Woman could make the meat last until Talking Elk killed again.

Boy watched Two Bears build a three-prong fish spear. The men had a fish spear when Boy and Fire Woman first met them. They had been catching large fish in a river and shared their good fortune with the two fugitives. Fire Woman and the boy helped dry some of the fish. The men were returning to their people from a long journey of exploring country far to the north where Two Bears' grandmother had grown up. They traded with the people there, but it was time to return to their own tribe before winter. On their way back they were following a river and decided to take a day to catch some of the large fish they had seen. Dried fish made good traveling food for their journey over the mountains.

All was lost when the young enemy warriors caught up to them and tried to recapture Fire Woman and the boy. Two Bears urged them to run and leave all they could not easily carry.

Two Bears had allowed Boy to try his new fish spear once. It was quite heavy for him, and he had missed the fish he aimed for. They tried to catch the fish along shallow, fast-moving parts of the river. Boy had been a bit afraid he would take an unwanted swim. Two Bears managed to catch several small fish so they had eaten again. Boy did not get another chance to try fishing with a spear. Once again, Two Bears' fish spear had been taken by the enemy.

Boy's thoughts of loneliness pushed his mind to the idea of leaving the cave, traveling to look for the woman's people who would take him in. It seemed the woman and he had been traveling for a very long time. She had stayed short times in different places, always avoiding others who the woman said would be enemies. She said they would be traveling many miles to find her people. They had found the men first.

Boy was unsure what to do. Where were the enemies who had killed Two Bears and taken the others? Would they find him before he found friendly people? He did not know if he would even know the woman's people should he find them. She had taught him some of her words, but he mostly had learned the words of his captors. Those words usually had been spoken in anger.

What about food and water? In the cave he had water. He had some food as well, but that wouldn't last too long. He had trapped all the resident rats months ago. The two men had been the meat hunters through the worst part of the winter. He didn't think he could get enough to eat whether he traveled or stayed. Which way would he go? He was not even sure which direction he had come from. Two Bears had known where this cave was and brought them there in a blizzard. What if the enemy came back?

He fell into a fitful sleep. His dreams were filled with images of the only three adults he had ever trusted trying to tell him things as they were being pulled away from him by unseen enemies.

CHAPTER TWO

Mother

The wolf knew she had lost her status in the pack, that of lead female, which she had fought hard to earn. Her mate had been the
pack leader. She was carrying his pups inside her, but the fight with a
bear over a kill brought a quick death to her mate. The bear had spun
and clamped his jaws down on her mate's neck when he had tried to
bite its flank. She had immediately reacted with a charge of her own,
but a swift paw had batted her clear of the fight circle, ripping the
tendon in her right rear leg. After that, she could only walk on three
legs. The pack had quit the fight with the bear shortly thereafter.

The remaining three strongest males had a fight of their own,
dominance was established, and a new male took leadership of the
pack. Other females competed to be the new leader's mate, and
once a new female had replaced her, the wounded wolf knew her
fate was sealed. The pack had no room for a cripple, and her pups
would be killed. Only the dominant pair was allowed to have a family
and all the other wolves would support them in that task.

She had stayed on the outskirts of the pack, only eating on a kill
after the rest had moved on and abandoned it. She was getting close
the time for her pups to come, and she knew she would have to
abandon the pack. The pack had already begun to ignore her. She
headed off into the forest, purposely moving to the outskirts of normal pack travel. She made note of good places to birth a litter of pups
as she searched for food. A plateau with tall grass held many small

27

rodents which were the staple of her diet now, being easier to catch than the larger game that the pack had hunted as a team. On the edge of the plateau was a ravine of rocky outcroppings with marmots. A larger rodent, the size of a month-old pup, this animal would provide several days' worth of meat if she could manage to wait one out and nab it unaware as it moved from one rock to another.

Down in the ravine, the trees of a forest grew, spreading with the width of the ravine, following a stream. This was the edge of the territory of her pack. She had not been there long when she heard another battle going on with the pack and a bear, further down the ravine. She was thankful to not be involved this time.

She inspected the fight scene a day or so later. There had been a fight among men before the bear had fought the wolves. She figured the old bruin had come to claim what spoils were there from the human battle and that the wolves had come patrolling their territory. The bear had a familiar smell. It had been the same old male that now had the scars of her mate's teeth on its ears and nose. This bear had a deep gravelly growl and was always itching for a fight. He was known to seek out the other predators to steal any food they might have killed and prove again he was the meanest predator in the forest. The old bruin reveled in another fight with the wolves. He seemed to enjoy the challenge. This bear was a menace. She was in no condition to have to fight him alone.

There were only blood stains on the rocks now. She noticed a large cave opening up the slope from where she stood, but she felt the need to move on. The fight was not that old and she didn't want to be caught lingering by any of the pack or the bear.

Something was not right in her belly. She knew it but did not know why. Several days later, she had found a shallow depression under a rock up on the plateau and dug it out a bit more. Her time was coming quickly, but she was weakening. She lay in the depression for a long time, licking morning dew from the surrounding grass as the only moisture within reach. Her pups finally came. Five pups in all, but only two were alive, one male and one female. She was now quite dehydrated and weak from the ordeal and the surviving pups were very vulnerable. The mother wolf needed to move them away from the dead pups as soon as possible. The smell would surely lure other predators. She picked up a wiggly pup by the saggy skin at the scruff of its neck, packing each of the siblings one by one fifty yards at a time, then returning for the second one so as not to abandon either for too long. The pups were blind, as canine pups are when born. They had a tawny yellow fur, soft and fluffy, nothing like they would look by the end of the summer when they grew in the grey and black colors of their adulthood.

She was still very weak and had to rest frequently. She knew that if the pups were to have a chance, she needed to conceal them. The cave she had seen before came to mind. It took her nearly all day to move her pups to the ravine. She curled around them to allow them to suckle and to keep them warm for the night. They fared well, but the exposure weakened her further as the nights were still cold. It took another half day to get both pups near the cave where she left them beneath a shallow outcropping of rocks and went forward to investigate.

The sky had turned dark and rain was imminent. She first checked for smells of the pack. She was relieved to find the sign was cold. The bear had found what he had wanted on the rocks below the cave and was long gone as well. She moved to the front of the cave where there was the smell of man, but it was not heavy. Of course, there would be man smell if men had occupied the cave for a while. There could even be man things left behind. If man still occupied the cave, there would be fresh smell of smoke, and probably a man on guard. None of these things were evident. The other wolves had been here briefly, but after the bear had moved on. There was no smell of bear in the cave. She decided to take a look inside. She worked her way along the south wall so as to keep her back protected from an enemy sneaking up behind her. She found no sign of man recently, but the smell still lingered. There was smell and signs that rodents visited the cave. That would be good for a close food source. And water. A small trickle of water ran out of the cave and there was a small pool the men had used for drinking. It was perfect.

Thunder rumbled and she flinched. Her back hurt tremendously and she wobbled on her one functional rear leg. She had to hurry. The day was dark with clouds obscuring the sun. The rain and wind picked up and blew hard. She forced herself to keep moving through her pain. Her pups' survival depended on it. They were too little to be exposed to the weather for long.

Under ordinary circumstances, she would have birthed them in a den dug into the ground, which would have been kept warm with soft fur she plucked from her own hide, but the pack would not have allowed her to return to the den she and her mate had dug. She was too weak to dig another. The cave would have to do.

Several hours later, she had managed to move both pups into the cave. She placed them on the north side away from the water and across from a rock shelf. She had a good view of the front of the cave from here in case a predator might enter. She drank a little and thought of her hunger.

Her thoughts turned to how she might feed her babies. Without her mate or other pack members to bring her meat, she would have to leave them to go hunt when they were still too small to be left. She curled herself around the pups once again and collapsed. The move had taken its toll. As she lay next to her tiny pups, they instinctively found her teats and began to suckle. She let sleep take her.

CHAPTER THREE

Wind in the Grass

The old scout was a master at his craft. His duty was to stay outside the safety perimeter of his tribe as they moved about to their favorite hunting or gathering grounds throughout the year. He watched for the enemy; he watched for the animals that hunters would hunt to feed the tribe. He studied all the animals and plants and their interactions.

As a scout, he stayed concealed even from his own tribal members. When he had something important to report, he hurried into the camp to a special lodge. His arrival was announced, and the elders gathered and listened to what he had to say. His job was one of the highest honors of the tribe. No scout ever told a lie, for that would cause the people to disbelieve what he had to say. That could prove fatal for him and his tribe. Afterwards, they would retire to a lodge where the women provided them with whatever they needed. Mostly it was a hot meal and a good night's rest or maybe a new pair of moccasins. It was an honor for the women of the tribe to help the scouts who sacrificed for the safety of them all.

Wind in the Grass was his name. He was given this name as a young man when an older warrior of his tribe witnessed an enemy scout who had been watching the tribe from too close. The warrior began sneaking closer to the enemy, but before he closed the distance, the squatting scout suddenly fell over backwards! When the warrior arrived, the enemy was already dead with his throat slit. The warrior looked around, but saw no clue as to what had killed him.

He began to check to see what the enemy might have of value when he heard a voice say: "Don't you think the warrior who defeats the enemy is entitled to the spoils?"

The older warrior spun around to see a young scout from his own tribe with a bloody knife in hand. The warrior, astonished that he had not seen the scout before, gladly let the young man claim the spoils. Upon returning to the village, he announced what he had witnessed. He told how this young man was so skilled at sneaking about unseen.

"All the enemy hears is the wind in the grass," the old warrior said. "By then, it is too late."

The people started calling the young scout Wind in the Grass that day, and his name never changed. The older warrior was long gone now, but the two tribesmen had remained friends for the rest of the warrior's life. Some of the young man's fellow scouts shortened his name to "Wind" when they talked amongst themselves.

"Wind" had seen over fifty-eight winters in his life and had spent over thirty of them protecting the tribe with his eyes, ears, nose, and an almost spiritual sense of what was moving in the world around him. He went out on his own and spent days or weeks living off the land and taking care of himself. His skill of survival was one of the best known to his tribe. It had to be. He was always in danger of encountering enemy tribes with nothing but his bow, hand axe, knife, and wits to keep from becoming an enemy warrior's bragging rights.

He traveled light. He had his clothing: moccasins, leggings, breechcloth, buckskin shirt, and sometimes a sleeping robe. He always packed some strong twine made of stinging nettle fibers for making traps, fish line, or whatever he might need. He also carried dry tinder for making a fire. He could make a fire board and find a hand drill to make a fire just about anywhere he went in his territory. He didn't often build a fire because the smell or the light at night could give away his location, but he had fire-making essentials in case of an emergency.

It was early spring and the tribe had moved to the foothills of the high mountains to hunt deer and to gather their favorite roots. Wind in the Grass was higher up the mountain following the trail of an enemy raiding party. He stayed back and only watched, as they were heading away from his tribe. It was a group of eight younger warriors, maybe sixteen to twenty winters old. He could tell the leader was trying to prove something by the way he treated the rest of the party.

"That one will die young," he thought to himself, suspecting that if he didn't act more like a leader than a bully, the rest of the young warriors might just let him earn the ultimate honor of falling in a battle.

Wind finally decided to turn back and let the warriors go as they headed over the mountain. He left their trail and headed cross country to a point above the plains where he could check on his tribe from a distance and determine if any other enemy might be lurking in the mountains above their hunting areas. A few days later, he returned and picked up the enemy trail. He wanted to be sure they had left the area. He tracked them down into a canyon where they had followed the river. Here on a rocky tumbledown of large rocks, he found the massacre. He read the tracks telling that a small group of people had been attacked.

They had probably been traveling and didn't have much for protective weapons. They had defended themselves from a cave part way up a steep rocky incline. A man a little older than himself lay dead on the rocks, his spear broken in two. Wind in the Grass didn't touch anything. The war party would have taken all that was of value, and besides, it may anger the spirits of the dead. He would claim only what was his right to claim in spoils of war, and he had no part in this battle. He did not recognize the look of the old man and could not determine his tribe. His spear was primitive without a stone point but rather, a fire-hardened tip. Wind figured that he had not possessed a bow and arrows. If he did, they had been stolen. Wind in the Grass had dealt with this man's enemy before.

Wind glanced inside the cave but got distracted when a large bear approached from below. He had wanted to read the sign around the old man one more time and cover him in rocks to show respect, but the bear already was upon the body. Wind left quickly.

The cave had been raided, and he wanted to determine which way the raiding party had gone. He found the place where one of the enemy warriors had been wounded. He hoped it was the leader who had exhibited an attitude towards his men when Wind had watched them earlier.

The raiders had left dragging someone, either a young adult male or a woman as the tracks indicated a smaller stature. He also found where a grown man had tracked the warriors and followed his trail. There was blood with this track too. This man had been wounded badly in the battle, and Wind wondered how far he had followed the men. The old scout found his answer two days later when he found the tracker's remains.

This man had a spear with a fire-hardened tip like the broken spear he'd found by the old man on the rocks. He had died trying to recapture his woman most likely, but she would be a slave in the hands of her enemies now. He wore buckskin clothing similar to Wind's own. His hairstyle showed he was of a tribe from the east. Wind had encountered these people and knew they were generally not found traveling in this area. The dead man carried a bone knife, some fire tinder, and dried food in a leather travel bag, but had no cloak or bed roll. He obviously had left in a hurry and probably did not have much with him when he was originally attacked. Wind knew the man's tribe had more sophisticated weapons, so this warrior must have known how to make them. Wind thought maybe he had been running with his woman and the old man from the enemy. They must have hidden in the cave when winter struck, and had to make the primitive spears in order to get food through the winter. If he had a bow and arrows, they must have been lost or stolen by this recent war party which had ultimately killed him. He wondered about their captive. She must have been some woman for these men to risk so much for her.

Wind had to return to his tribe and tell them what he had seen. He took the time to cover the man with rocks. It would keep the scavengers off his body. Wind thought this must have been an honorable warrior to try so hard to save his woman. He left the spear stuck upright in the ground as a monument but buried the rest of the man's gear with him. The warrior's spirit would need them in the next life.

Wind in the Grass told the elders of what he had seen and they kept an eye out for the marauders. As spring became summer, the tribe moved on to their summer camps further east. They participated in a large summer gathering with related tribes before returning the way they had come. In late summer they would head for their wintering camps south of the mountains on the banks of a wide, slow-moving river.

CHAPTER FOUR

Uneasy meeting

Boy awoke from a fitful sleep. Rain was splatting on the side of the mouth of the cave, dripping onto the rock floor with a "splish" sound. A roar came from outside made by heavy rain driven by wind onto the rocky hillside. He knew it was morning instinctively, even though the lighting was dimmed by the storm. He shuffled his feet as he began to move out from under the rock shelf. He heard a whining noise and froze. Could the four-legged hunters have returned?

He carefully peered out and saw a full-grown wolf lying across the cave from him, apparently asleep. It was mostly grey, but the ridge of its back was black and its belly a bit whiter. Its tail was fluffy but lay still on the ground. The ears were relaxed and faced toward the front of the cave; its eyes were closed. It wasn't moving much but whining noises were coming from it. He decided to wait and watch. He waited most of the day. It had only shifted positions where it lay, but had not got up and moved.

Boy was very thirsty. He slid as silently as he could from under the shelf to the water, took a quick drink, and shoved himself back, expecting the wolf right behind him. The wolf remained lying down. He looked at the wolf. The wolf's large yellow eyes locked with his. It was staring at him with piercing intent. The fur on the back of its neck was standing up and its ears were laid back. A low grumble began deep within its chest. He scrunched himself back under the shelf as far as he could go. He pulled out a bit of dried meat and ate it. He had to wait the wolf out until it got bored and left.

The wolf saw the movement from the corner of her eye. She thought at first of a marmot or even a badger, but that was not it. It came out and drank water and then slid back under the shelf. She immediately thought of her pups. Would they be in danger? She was no match for a badger in her weakened condition. But then the smell hit her nose. Man! It was a man! Her hair stood up and she began to growl. She stared intently into the darkness under the rock shelf. Man could be very dangerous, but this one was small and evidently alone. In her full health she could have waited it out and killed it by herself. But now she knew she was dying. She did not have the strength to even raise her head for very long, let alone stand and fight. She needed food, but she could not hunt. Without her, the pups would die. Her growl trailed off, and her hair laid flat again. She stared out the front of the cave to the forest beyond. Her thoughts wandered to the joy she had felt running through those trees, hunting as the lead female of her pack.

The boy watched all day and into the night. He could no longer see the wolf, but he knew it was there. He would have to wait until daylight again. Long days and nights hiding under the shelf were taking a toll on Boy. His legs were cramping, and he needed to get up and move about. He needed another drink too, but couldn't risk it with the wolf out there. He resigned himself to wait, but he didn't get much sleep. The next morning he could see the wolf hadn't moved. That seemed strange for a large predator. The whining had become more intense through the night, but the wolf was silent now.

Boy went for another drink. After his quick move out and back, he looked at the wolf but its eyes were closed. He thought maybe it had died in the night. He grabbed his spear and inched out from under the rock. He thought about running, but where could he go? He figured he would run the spear through the apparently sleeping wolf. If it was already dead, then so be it. If it was alive, he would have a fight on his hands, so he'd better make the first throw good. The big wolf's eyes were still closed. It had not reacted to his movements. He quietly circled it for a better angle.

That's when he noticed two tiny fluff balls nuzzling up to the belly of the grown wolf. Boy was shocked. His plan of action was instantly undermined. He had to think again. He saw the wolf in a whole new light. She was not waiting to kill him. She was sick and trying to protect her pups. The pups were so young that their eyes were still closed and they made quiet whining noises.

Backing out towards the mouth of the cave, Boy stood in the sun watching the wolf and thinking. Was she already dead? Her head shook a bit, her eyes opened, and she breathed deeply. No, she was still alive, but Boy also knew she wasn't well. What did she need? Probably food and water just like he did. He moved back into the cave, retrieved his food bag from under the rock shelf, and tossed a scrap of dried meat near the wolf's nose. She immediately opened her eyes and sniffed. She tried to reach the meat but was too weak. Boy moved closer and used his short spear to push the dried meat toward her. She greedily ate the meat without raising her head.

He felt very sympathetic to her situation. She was stranded like he was, but he could hardly afford to share what little dried meat he had. He wondered what he would do when it ran out. He walked outside the cave and looked around. He went down the trail and found plants he knew he could eat, and gathered some roots and old leaves. He ate his fill and gathered some more. He looked around but didn't see anything else he could use. He wondered if the wolf ate leaves. He could eat leaves for a while. They were not always the best tasting but they were plentiful and as spring came on, the new leaves would taste better and be even more available. He also knew that the plant that grew by the river with long stems and the long leaves, the one used to weave mats, had a small yellow head on it in the spring. It could be eaten along with parts of the roots.

Fire Woman had taught him these things and now that he needed them, her lessons were coming back. He planned to visit the river on another day to gather what he could find.

On the way back to the cave a mouse scurried across the path. The string! Of course! He could trap mice as he had trapped rats last winter. The wolf would definitely eat mice. There wasn't much meat there, but with spring new families of mice would be moving about and gathering food themselves. That would be one thing he could hunt himself.

The lessons of Two Bears were coming back to him. They had eaten rats when they first reached the cave. Two Bears also had shown Boy how to tie a string to a short stick, balance a flat rock on the stick, and set the trap on a rodent trail in the cave. When the rat passed under the rock, he could jerk the string, causing the rock to fall and kill the rodent. He had kept the cave free of mice and packrats in this manner. Fire Woman had cooked the rodents in a stew, and they had shared what she made. Boy had spent a lot of time tearing down the rats' nests, stacking the wood near the fire, and trapping the rats that ran out. It was Boy who discovered the back room of the cave. He had crawled back there looking for more wood, and found what he was looking for, but also something he hadn't expected. Under the rats' nest were three holes in the ground. Three flat rocks once had covered them but had been pushed off to one side. They were filled with wood and fur and leaves that the rats had brought in.

Boy used the wood and over time hollowed out each hole. Inside the holes he could see where they had been made carefully with rocks and hard mud. The rocks stacked up with mud and dry grass filled in between and smoothed out by the maker's hands. He could put his little fingers in the prints of the grandfather who had built it so long ago. Two bears said it was a storage bin meant to keep the rats out of their winter food. The grandfathers must have lived there a long time. But they had also been gone for a long time.

Boy was excited about the prospect of trapping the mice that were coming out in the warmer weather. He hurried on up to the cave entrance but moved inside slowly. He didn't fully trust the situation

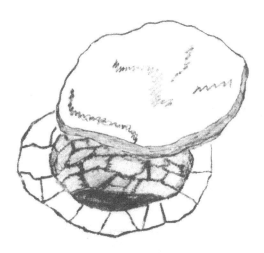

with the wolf even though it seemed she was too weak to move. She had tried to move, maybe to reach the water. Boy considered how he could stay far enough away and yet get water to her.

He reached under the shelf and brought out the string. He went back outside and down the hill. There he found a large, flat rock and broke a short stick from a dead tree limb. He lugged them up near the mouth of the cave, where the mouse trail went from tall grass to a crack in the rocks. Boy set the flat rock over the trail. He tied the end of the string to the middle of the stick then propped up one edge of the rock with the end of the stick. He was careful to put a smaller, fist-sized rock under the edge of big flat one while he balanced it on the end of the stick. Two Bears had shown Boy his scars from the mistake of not setting a safety stone and squashing his fingers with his own trap.

Once the trap was set, Boy backed off to the edge of the cave where he could watch the mouse trail. He pulled up the slack on the string and then laid it down. It would be a while before the mouse returned, so he went back inside to consider how to bring water to the wolf. He didn't want to get too close to the wolf's head, but she couldn't move much and he couldn't move her.

The pool of water was at least as far from the wolf's head as its body was long but within the boy's arm's length from the edge of his rock shelf. He needed something to carry water to her. He didn't know how to make something to carry water in. The containers Fire Woman cooked with had been stolen. He looked around again. He followed the stream of water out of the cave and looked down the waterfall. Attached to the hill were large rocks with depressions that held water. Maybe he could find a smaller rock that he could carry. He climbed down the steep part of the hill, following the water. He walked into the forest to where the little stream joined another. If he kept following the stream he would reach the river, but he didn't want to go that far. He did walk farther than he had planned. The plight of the wolf was giving Boy a reason to get out and do something. And doing something to help the wolf was helping him start to find what he needed to survive.

There it was! The rock he was looking for. It was about as big around as his head but flat on the bottom and only his hand width tall. Most importantly, the top had a depression. Not much of one, but it held some water. He picked it up. It was a bit heavier than the rock he had gathered for his trap. He followed a game trail back to his eating plants, then up the hill. He avoided the grassy area where his trap was set. When he returned to the cave, he took the stone to the water pool but kept an eye on the mother wolf. Using his cupped hands, he filled the depression with water. With the blunt end of his short spear, he pushed the whole rock close enough so she could drink.

She now had to lift her head to get a drink, but the smell of the water so close gave her strength and she managed to do it.

Mother Wolf had awakened again when the small man had crawled out from the rock to drink. She was too weak to acknowledge him. She had been aware he was circling her and was resigned to die a failure to her pups. Her eyelids were heavy. She wanted to sleep. The pups just kept suckling her and whined their disapproval at the small amount of milk her teats offered.

This was the way of the wild. Every animal fought for its own survival. The pack had killed other animals to feed its members, but then every animal knew it too must die in turn. Mother Wolf decided it was her time. She had given up. The blow she expected never came. She never would understand that it was her pups that had saved her. Man could kill yes, but man also had empathy for others, especially when man could identify with their plight. The small man had stopped in the middle of his attack preparation. The next thing she knew he had tossed her a bit of dry, but good-smelling meat. It reminded her of the way her wolf mother had tossed her small mice when she was a pup. This was unlike any human she had ever encountered.

The small amount of food did wonders for her. Although she was dehydrated and needed water, the food in her belly gave her the slightest bit of hope. She could feel her pups moving next to her. She was curious, but cautious about this small man.

When she wasn't sleeping, she watched as he busied himself going to and from the cave. He watched her as well, and he didn't get too close. That suited her just fine. And best of all, he never tried to get close to her pups. That she would not tolerate.

Then the small human did another unexpected thing. He brought in a rock that could hold some water and pushed it close enough for her to drink. This small human was definitely not like any others. He was special, caring for her as if he were part of her pack. She was feeling better. She would let this human help her. If she survived, then her pups would survive. For that, she could live in the same cave with man. At least, with this man.

Boy had to push the rock bowl back and forth with his spear several times before the mother wolf had stopped lapping up the water. He left the last one full while she appeared to sleep. He grabbed his wolf skin robe and went out to the edge of the cave mouth and sat down near the end of his string. It was late in the afternoon now and he figured the rodents would be moving. He sat for what seemed like a long time watching the trap and thinking of his people. Two Bears was dead, he knew that. He had seen the blood stains and had found his broken spear. He remembered watching Two Bears sharpen the hard wood shaft and then harden it in the evening fire. He missed the fire. He thought how odd it was that they had kept the fire not only for warmth but to keep predators such as wolves away from the cave. Now he found himself caring for a sick wolf in that very cave. He figured Two Bears would not approve.

Talking Elk and Fire Woman were gone. No sign of them. He figured they were probably dead as well. They had not returned in several days. They would have come to get him if they could. He felt the sadness seep into his bones.

Just then a movement caught his eye. A large mouse ran under his trap. He had not been paying attention, so he had missed his opportunity. The mouse had gone from the rock to the grass. He waited and watched more intently. He didn't have to wait long. The mouse came back packing a mouth full of grass. He didn't make it past the trap this time. Boy jerked the string and "thump!" the flat rock crushed the mouse. Boy rushed to his trap and lifted the rock to claim his bloody prize. He set the trap again then went into the cave.

His excitement got the best of him and he said boldly: "Look, wolf! I caught you some dinner!"

He tossed the mouse to the wolf. She devoured it, this time lifting her head a little. Boy returned to his trap and caught another mouse before dark. This time he pulled the skin off and ate the raw flesh of the legs himself. It tasted good. He was used to eating meat raw, and usually did when his people had made a fresh kill. They then would dry a lot of the meat so it would not spoil. Boy tossed the remaining bits to wolf who seemed pleased to eat them as well.

Mother Wolf was awakened suddenly by the loud thump of the trap rock falling against the hard ground. She was startled again by the loud noises the human made when he came in to her. He wasn't growling and he wasn't howling. He sounded more like a pack of those pesky ravens than anything else. He was obviously excited about something, but she didn't know if it meant danger or something else. Then he tossed her the bloody mouse.

"He's been hunting," she thought.

And he had tossed the whole thing to her. Another wolf would have eaten all or part of the kill first, especially a kill this small.

It was accepted in the pack that the hunters would eat first because it was their strength that kept them hunting for others. Only after a hunter had eaten would the weak be allowed to feed. This human was treating her better than her own pack would have. She looked at him as he sat by the cave entrance. This small man was no danger to her or her pups. She would try to regain her strength and raise her pups. She heard the trap snap again. This time she noticed the human ate first.

"Good," she thought. "That makes more sense."

She still was happy to receive a portion.

Boy set the trap rock up on the safety rock to let mice run under it all night and get used to the flat rock being there. He rolled up the string and brought it onto the cave with him. String was much too valuable to have some critter run off with it in the night or chew it in two. He gave the wolf another series of drinks and left the rock with water in it so she could get to it in the night. He still crawled under his stone shelf to sleep after eating a bit of the roots he had gathered and had a drink for himself from the pool. He wasn't sure he wanted to fall asleep where the wolf could reach him if she suddenly recovered.

CHAPTER FIVE

Friendship

Boy slept well that night. So did Mother Wolf. The previous day's encounters had set both their minds at ease. Boy woke with a purpose. He checked on the wolf. She had moved her head and curled up around her babies a bit but still wasn't standing.

He brought her some more water then moved out to the mouth of the cave and reset the trap. He caught a couple mice in the morning, but as the sun came full up the mice had disappeared into the rocks to carry on their daytime activities under cover. Boy gathered more roots and leaves and this time left some for the wolf along with her share of the mice. The wolf never ate the plants, and they were there at the end of the day. Boy was getting more comfortable with the wolf and had even moved the water rock with his hand once, not thinking about the danger. The wolf had only moved to drink, not to bite him. He was beginning to trust her a bit more. She already trusted him.

A week passed and the boy got more efficient with his trap. He had to move its position several times but was still catching mice. He climbed up on the rim above the cave and found a marmot trail where the marmot colony lived and set a bigger trap up with a safety rock to let the marmots get used to it. He would be back to wait for a chance there in a few days. Boy noticed the plants were greening up. The good weather had encouraged growth, and new leaves were available to eat.

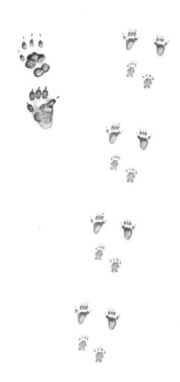

He had been saving as much of the dried meat as he could now that fresh meat was available. He realized that the wolf had not growled since the first time she saw him, and he observed the pups were moving around more.

Mother Wolf felt much better. She was still weak but could hold her head up and lick her pups. She hadn't stood up on her three good legs since the night she came to the cave, and her hips still hurt when she tried. She could drag herself to the water and back now. And that gave her a feeling of accomplishment. The human noticed and didn't bother with the water rock anymore. He spent more of his time out hunting with his loud snapping rock. She was surprised at how well he hunted with it. She noticed the excitement in his jabbering when he came in with the first marmot.

She watched while he carefully skinned it. He had a sharp rock he held in his paws. His paws were not like her paws. They could wrap around things and hold them, but he had very poor claws. She figured he couldn't dig a hole anywhere near as fast as she could, well, as she used to. The human used the sharp rock to cut up the marmot meat. He ate some and gave some to her. There was enough to help satisfy her increasing hunger, and save some for later. He even set some out on the rocks in the sun. She wondered why he would risk a bird or a rodent getting it like that. She would have eaten it all if she were the hunter. She knew she was growing stronger each day.

Boy remembered helping Fire Woman dry meat for storage. They had built racks for the meat and a fire to smoke the meat as it dried. Smoke flavored the meat and kept the flies away. He did not have a fire now, or know how to make one. He dried the meat on the warm rocks in the sun. He had watched Fire Woman make a fire once or twice, but for the most part, the fire was always kept warm enough to blow into flame when they needed it. He had blown the fire into flame many times and could do that again if he had any coals. He missed the fire.

He discovered that in order to dry in the sun, the meat had to be cut really thin. He watched closely to make sure birds and rodents didn't steal it. He had to bring it in at night, then set it out again when the sun was up. By drying the slices of meat, he could make one marmot last for several days.

He was also drying the hide of the marmot by pinning it stretched out on the dirt with small sharpened sticks and letting it dry.

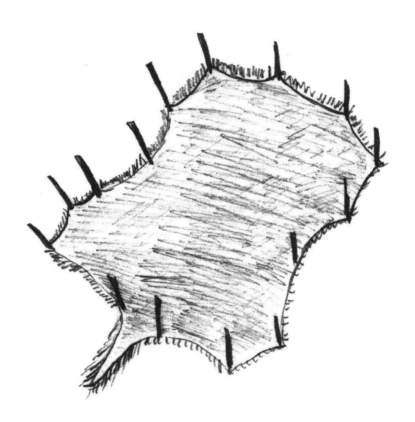

He could then cut a spiral pattern out of it carefully with the pointed sharp end of his stone blade. He had watched Two Bears do this to make rawhide string which was strong enough to tie sticks together to make drying racks and other useful things. The hides that were not used, he stacked in the back of the cave for later. He didn't know how to make them soft like Fire Woman had, but he figured they had value anyway.

Weeks passed. Mother Wolf grew stronger. The pups opened their eyes and began to explore their surroundings. Boy sat and watched them in the middle of the day when hunting was poor. They were hilarious with their wrestling and chasing each other. They were also making more noise. If they got out of hand, Mother Wolf nipped them to put them back in line. Boy also noticed she was chewing up her meat and then regurgitating it back up for her pups. The pups seemed to really enjoy it. He thought this unappetizing, but figured that wolves had their own ways. And the pups were getting bigger so it must have been working.

One day while Boy was sitting quietly on the rock shelf, the male pup, who was getting good with his short little runs across the cave, bounded across the cave floor and leapt into his lap! Mother Wolf saw it happening and it scared her. What would the human do? Would he kill the pup? Her instinct was protective and she rose up on her three good legs in a full-height standing position. The man saw her reaction and although he was cackling like those ravens again, he simply put the pup down facing the mother wolf and let go. The pup bounded between his mother's legs and nipped at her tail as he went by. He located his sister and sent her rolling in a full body attack.

Mother Wolf just stared at the human and he stared back but he wasn't excited. He was making his noises in a calm voice. She suddenly realized she was standing. She was very pleased and surprised with herself so she carefully took some wobbling steps over to the water pool and took a drink. Then she moved back to her resting place and lay down again. She looked around at the pups. They didn't seem to know or care if they had put themselves in the hands of another predator. Mother Wolf was satisfied with the outcome of the incident.

Boy had been twisting a rawhide spiral into the rawhide cord he was making, when out of nowhere a little fur ball landed right in the middle of him.

"Oh!" he laughed. "What are you up to, little one?"

He picked him up high and looked at the pup, but then he realized Mother Wolf had stood up for the first time since he had met her and she was staring right at his eyes. He understood immediately her concern with her pup and turned the pup toward her and set him back down. The pup immediately raced for his mother.

Boy talked to Mother Wolf in a gentle voice: "It's OK. I will not hurt your babies. But look at you! You are standing up. You must be getting better!"

It suddenly occurred to Boy that he may now be in danger if she could stand again. The feeling made him uneasy. He also noticed that one of her rear legs had been injured and had healed in a deformed position. It was scarred and mangled and she didn't put any weight on it. He wondered how it got like that, but that just made him think how tough she must be to survive all the setbacks she had been through. He didn't want to believe that she would hurt him, but then they were natural enemies and competing predators. He began working on his string again, keeping an eye on her. She relaxed and wobbled over to get a drink and wobbled back to lie back down again. Boy grinned. He had helped her get her feet back, and she had given him reason to keep going. He was pleased with the way things were.

The next week went by and the pups were not going to let their mother rest. They saw no reason not to include Boy in their rough housing. He had always been a member of the pack as far as they knew, and he seemed to be doing all of the hunting for the pack. Obviously, he was fair game. Mother Wolf watched intently the first few times, but the human continued to act like one of the pack letting the pups nip at him while showing great patience and even pleasure with their attention.

She was moving around more, and even though her hips still hurt, she was walking on her three good legs. She even found herself moving closer to the human voluntarily. His constant successful hunting earned him the right to be a part of their small pack even if he was human. As days passed, she felt the urge to hunt again herself, and began leaving the cave at night. She wouldn't go far, just enough to listen to the night sounds and explore the smells of her surroundings. Once in a while she heard a mouse busily gathering seeds to store for the winter and managed to pounce on it before it got away. She ate some and the other she took back to feed to her pups as they were growing strong teeth and needed the whole mouse to chew. Mother Wolf became more trusting of the boy, enough to leave her pups with him while she went out. She knew he stayed in the cave at night, and the pups would curl up and sleep with him.

As Mother grew stronger, she traveled farther at night, sometimes bringing in a grouse or a fat tree squirrel. Her hunting took the pressure off Boy to feed her, and in turn, the pups. Boy still hunted and dried the meat as best he could in the sun. He stuffed his food bag again with the dried meat and stashed it for later in case he couldn't hunt. The mice and the pups were constantly trying to get into his food stash, so he moved the food and the rawhide box to one of the storage bins in the back of the cave. He pulled the rock over the opening and left it there until he needed it. As his hunting success improved and the storage bin proved tight, he began filling it with marmot meat.

Mother Wolf began staying out all night. She returned and slept during the day, watching her pups while the boy left to hunt and gather what he could. The boy always packed his short spear with him. It was the one real weapon he owned. It was a simple hardwood shaft with the end pointed and hardened in a fire. He had scraped it sharp a few times after having practiced throwing it at bushes. Two Bears had taken time to dry and harden it just so, and then scrape it smooth to feel good in his hand. It had to have taken great force to break it. As it was now, it was just the right length for the boy, standing as tall as he was on its end. It was a bit heavy, but he didn't care. It had belonged to a man he admired and respected.

Boy liked to gather leaves in the morning when Mother was still out and the pups were still lethargic. He had gone down below the cave to his favorite bush for leaves. The sun was just rising. The morning dew was evaporating off the rock slide in front of the cave creating a fog that obscured the sun but promised a warm day.

He was enjoying his vegetable breakfast when his hair suddenly stood up on the back of his neck. A chill ran down his spine. He was suddenly afraid, but he didn't know why. He cautiously headed back up to the cave entrance, watching all directions anticipating an attack. As he eased around the corner of the cave entrance, he saw a large mountain cat hunched over a pup!

CHAPTER SIX

Mountain Lion

The pups had been rough housing as normal after they awoke and found themselves alone. The female pup had gone to the cave entrance and looked down the hill to see the boy. She turned and ran back into the cave. The male pup bowled her over and she ran for cover under the sleeping shelf. He was about to follow when a large mountain lion bounded into the cave. The male spun out of the way of the sharp claws but was batted across the cave floor. Finding his feet, he scurried under the rock shelf. The cat was there in an instant, reaching with its claws extended trying to grab one of the pups. The male pup growled and nipped at the clawed appendage. He was rewarded with a quick upturn of the big paw and was caught by the ear on two of the cat's claws. The cat began dragging the male pup out from under the rock shelf, but his sister ran forward and bit the cat on the face just as the male pup broke free by ripping his ear loose. The cat wasted no time and had the female in its mouth quickly, killing her instantly. The male barked loudly as the cat began to back away.

Boy realized the cat had one of the pups. His fear turned to rage as the feeling of protecting his only family welled up inside him. He hurled his short spear at the center of the cat's chest. It struck and penetrated deeply. The cat whirled on the spear, biting it as hard as he could, rolling and twisting into all sorts of contortions until the spear fell out. The cat stopped momentarily to look in the direction the spear came from, but looking into the light at the mouth of the cave, it overlooked the boy now hunkered down to the edge of the cave. Two quick leaps and the cat was gone.

The boy rushed to the pup, grabbed her in his arms, and slipped under the rock shelf with the now bleeding male. They scrunched to the back of his sleeping area and he pulled both pups to him. He didn't realize the female was already dead.

The boy did not know how lucky he had been with his throw. The cat had been sideways to him and slightly facing away. Boy's spear had entered just behind the cat's rib cage and penetrated forward, piercing a lung. The mountain lion ran from the cave and down the hill to the trees, disappearing into the forest to the east. If the spear had been a bit farther back, wounded or not, the cat may have had enough air in its lungs to catch a small human.

As Mother Wolf bounded into the cave on her three good legs, her fur was standing up. She was prepared to do battle, but the battle was over. She had been up on the ridge when she heard a sound she had not heard before. It was definitely made by the boy, but he was mad or scared or both. She took off running to protect her pack. She looked around and saw that there was no immediate threat. She could smell the cat and trailed its blood to the cave entrance, but there were other blood smells here too.

The male pup bounded out of the boy's arms when it saw its mom. His head was bloody and his ear had been ripped into three distinct pieces still attached at the base. He was OK, just sore. His ear would never look the same.

As the boy crawled out, he laid the female pup on the cave floor. He could see now she was gone. Mother Wolf sniffed her and licked her for a while, then lay down beside her stretched out with her head on her paws and watching her dead pup. The boy walked across the cave and picked up the spear that had fallen from the cat as it scrambled. It had blood on it, from the tip down the shaft the length of Boy's forearm. He packed it back and sat down beside Mother Wolf. Mother sniffed the spear tip then went back to watching the pup.

Mother had assessed the problem quickly. She knew that the boy had speared the cat and had driven it away. She had checked the male pup's wounds. He was going to be OK. Her female pup, though, was dead. Mother watched it anyway to see if there were any signs of life.

After a while she gently picked up the little broken puppy by the scruff of the neck and left the cave. She didn't return until after dark. When she did, she didn't have the pup. That night she sat on the ridge top and howled mournfully.

The next day she stayed close and licked the male pup's ears clean. Boy stayed close too and had his spear at the ready. Mother understood his feelings of fear and responsibility. She had those same feelings now and before when she was the lead female of a pack. The male pup was lethargic all day and slept in the boy's lap. They were all sad, and did not feel like doing much.

Boy washed his body clean of blood from holding the dead puppy. He even scraped the floor to remove the blood stains. It was depressing to see them there, but he left the cat blood to dry on his spear. It was a reminder as well, but there was a bit of pride in that stain.

CHAPTER SEVEN

Training Pup

The next day Mother left the cave in broad daylight. She walked slowly and looked back, encouraging the pup to follow. He eventually did follow, and she took him out on his first foray away from the cave. She took him up on the bench above the cave and out into the meadow where she had been hunting mice. The pup watched intently and when she caught her first one by sitting still and listening for its movements, the pup finally knew what she was up to. She tossed him the partially wounded mouse and let him play with it. Instinct runs deep in wild creatures. Just as the boy knew he must make meat and save it for worse times, the pup knew he must learn to hunt and put on weight as his mother did. The pup's official schooling had begun.

The trips became more frequent and longer. The pup began losing his tan baby hair and was getting a silvery coat of a young adult. He still played too much and was not attentive to the dangers in the world but snapped right to attention if his mom nipped him to let him know he should be aware of what is going on around him.

The boy found more time on his hands. The leaves he liked to eat were not as fresh anymore, but berries were coming on and he watched them grow. He realized he would need something to carry them when they ripened so he could dry them for storage. He didn't know how to weave a basket like Fire Woman had made, but he had lots of marmot skins. He sat down with his knife and a sharp stick. He trimmed one hide to leave it as large as he could but cut off the legs

63

so it had more of a square shape to it. He took another hide and trimmed it the same size. He was forming a plan. He soaked the hides in the water, then poked holes with a sharp stick around the skin, spacing them about the width of his little finger. He took some of the rawhide cord he had twisted up on a ball, soaked it in water until it became soft, and then began stitching the two together, in one hole and out the next. He wasn't sure how to tie off the end, so he left it a hand's length longer and cut it off. Using the tails of the rawhide string, he sewed back overlapping the previous stitches which strengthened the top joint of hides and hid the tails of the rawhide string without a large knot. In the process of sewing, he had made his seams on the outside of the bag, and the hair ended up on the inside. His bag had dried considerably and was hard and stiff. He was pleased with his new gathering bag. It would work even if the hair was on the inside.

He was tired of sewing, so he took his new bag and his spear and headed east toward the river on a foraging expedition. He didn't go there often due to his constant need to hunt for meat, but the water was becoming more fascinating as he had the time to do other things. He could see small fish in the pools of the river, but he had no idea how to catch them. Two Bears and Talking Elk had used long spears with three serrated prongs on the end to stab big fish and wrestle them to the shore where Fire Woman cut them into strips and dried them over the fire or made a soup with them in a big leather bag. She had filled the bag with water then put the fish parts and hot rocks in the bag. She would swap rocks from the bag to the fire and back again until the soup was bubbling hot. He missed fire. He missed Fire Woman and her cooking.

Walking along the edge of the creek, he spotted a crayfish in a small pool off the side of the river. He reached in and grabbed it, tossing it on the ground. He poked at it with his spear tip. Its claws came up in a defensive position. He remembered eating these as well. They had been cooked, but he thought he would try eating it raw. He picked up a stone and crushed its outer shell, killing it. He then used his thumb to scrape out the tail meat. He ate it but grimaced at the taste. It wasn't anywhere near as good as it had been when cooked. He looked in the claws for more meat but didn't find enough to worry about. He tossed the rest of the dead crayfish back into the river. He figured other crayfish would eat the rest.

He walked along and looked for anything else he might use or eat. He began wondering if his gathering bag would hold water like Fire Woman's cooking bag. He looked at it but decided it wouldn't hold water because it had too many stitching holes. He wondered how she had made her cooking bag water tight. He sat down in the sun and leaned against a rock. It was hot so he decided to go swimming. He wasn't a good swimmer. He had never been taught properly. That would have happened when the men took him out. He laughed thinking that was exactly what the wolves were doing now. The pup was going out on the hunt as Boy would have if the men were still here. The pup would earn a name before Boy would! He wondered if wolves did that sort of thing. Boy decided he would name the pup. He would look for a sign that would tell him what the name should be. With that thought, he jumped in the river. It was cold but felt good. He got his long hair wet and ran his fingers through it getting the dirt out. He stayed in as long as he could before the cold got to him. Then he laid himself out on a large boulder to let the sun dry him.

He had fallen asleep in the sun and woke with a start. He couldn't let that happen when he was out away from the safety of the cave. He had to stay always aware of what was going on around him. He listened but heard nothing out of the ordinary. He grabbed his bag and spear and headed back closer to the cave. He was thinking about the fishing spear, and he looked for a long willow shoot stout enough to make one. He found a suitable one. He looked around and found a large stone with a sharp edge.

There were always many more handy stones down by the river. A lot of them were rounded off like Fire Woman's cooking stones, but some had jagged edges. He had to watch out he didn't cut himself on the sharp ones. He had always been barefoot in the warm months, and he walked putting his toes down first and letting his heel come down slowly. That way he could feel a jagged rock or a thorny stick before he put his full weight upon his foot. He also walked quieter this way.

He found the stone he needed to use as a hand axe and chopped off the long willow shoot. It was twice as long as he stood high. He cut three equal-length prongs out of another willow shoot. Using his bag, he carried the hand axe and prongs back to the cave.

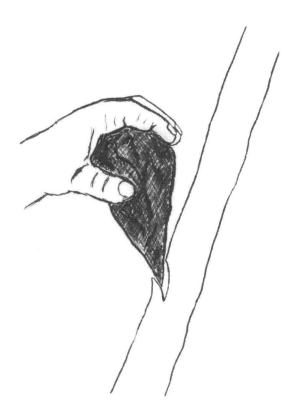

This bag was going to come in handy. The problem he found was the bag had dried stiff and flat. He pried it open with the sticks and forced the rock down inside. He would have to work on that.

Heading back toward the cave, he took a shortcut through the trees. Suddenly he froze. There in front of him curled up under the low-hanging branches of a tree was the big cat.

CHAPTER EIGHT

Claws

The cat appeared to be sleeping. The boy's hatred for the cat over-took him. He dropped his bag and willow stick in the process of rushing the cat with his spear. He jabbed the cat hard! He pulled back his spear and stabbed the cat over and over. The cat never moved, and had a bad smell to it as well. Once he had calmed down, he realized the cat was already dead. He turned it over. Its whole side was covered in dried blood from his original spear throw. The cat was big, but it didn't seem as big now as it had in the cave. The boy thought to himself that if the men were here they would be proud of Boy killing a big predator, and they would give him a real name. They also would make a necklace out of a claw and hang it around his neck to show others he had killed a big cat.

Boy decided to make his own necklace and used his knife to at-tempt to cut off one of the cat's claws. The knife scratched the base of the claw but wasn't cutting it. So the boy moved his blade further up on the paw and cut through the flesh. He found that if he cut at the knuckle joint, the bones would separate with less work. He fin-ished cleaning off the flesh and had a nice-looking claw to work with. He decided to take another and did so, but by that time he was tired of the process. He put the two claws into his carry bag.

When he arrived back at the cave both Mother and wolf pup were there. Mother was napping, but the pup bounded up to inspect what the boy had brought back. He smelled the cat on him and growled. The boy let the pup sniff the bag and his hand. Although the

69

pup didn't like what he smelled, he figured there must not be any danger because the boy was there and seemed OK.

He lay down close to Boy and watched as the boy took the tip of his knife and began drilling a hole in one of the claws. It took quite a while, and he had to drill from both sides but eventually he broke through. He then took a small stick and ran it through the opening to round out the hole. He then used some of the string that Fire Woman had made, cutting just enough to hang the claw around his neck. He strung the claw, tied off the ends, and pulled it over his head. The way he had drilled the claw made it poke into his chest so he reversed the way he wore it so it hung with the curve of the claw pointing out. He was proud to wear it. It represented his first major kill. Now he could call himself a hunter.

He crawled under his sleeping shelf and set the second claw on a shallow ledge at the back. He wasn't sure what he would use it for but that would keep the pup from carrying it off.

Boy set out to try to build a fish spear. He had remembered the three-pronged fishing spear the men had used to catch fish the summer they had met. He had enough marmot skin to make rawhide lashing, so he started by cleaning up the long spear he had cut. He trimmed off any little branches with the chopping rock. He then went outside the cave and found a smaller rock with a sharp, broken edge. He used that to scrape the green bark off the shaft and also to scrape the ends of the shaft smooth. He set the spear along the cave wall to stiffen as it dried. Scraping the bark off the three short sticks, he sharpened them and began to carve notches in them. The notches created barbs that faced the inside of a triangle formed between the three prong tips. They would help hold a fish on if he were to spear one. The barbs started from right behind the tip to three quarters of the way up each point. This was a lot of carving. He didn't finish the first one before nightfall, so he set the project aside for another time. When darkness came, Boy curled up in his robe and Pup curled up next to him. Mother went out for her evening hunt.

During the night Pup got up and wandered around the cave. He missed his sister and the rough housing. The boy was always busy and never seemed to want to wrestle like she had. He found the bag the boy had made and chewed on it a bit. He packed it back and forth and eventually tired of it. When he dropped it, it fell plunk in the little pool for drinking water. Pup didn't care and went off to see if he could hear Mother coming back. Eventually he curled up next to the boy again and slept until morning.

When morning came Mother was still out. She had gone farther south than before. She had traveled to the edge of the forest overlooking flat lands that stretched for miles. They were not really all that flat, what with little draws and canyons to hide in, but from up on the mountain where she was, it looked flat.

Out on the prairie she found signs of many bigger meat animals. She had been there before and recognized the scent of the pronghorn antelope. They were very fast. It would take a whole pack of wolves with all four legs to hunt them. An antelope had to be run with one hunter taking over when the previous hunter tired. The pack would take turns until the pronghorn would tire and give the hunters a chance to rip a tendon in its hind legs. That would stop it and the kill could be made. She and her pup would not be able to chase down a pronghorn anytime soon.

Elk were present, but again it took several wolves to bring down even a small one. Before a kill could be made, the mother elk had to be distracted while a young one was chased away from its herd. Hunting elk was out of her reach at this time too. Hunting alone she might be able to kill a young mule deer, but she would have to be wary of its mother. Mother deer were fiercely protective and had sharp hooves to stomp a hunter.

She followed the first fresh smell of deer and found herself wandering in what would be a daytime bedding ground. The deer were out feeding or bedding in the tall grass now. She followed the scent trail back the other direction and came to an open meadow. The deer would be out there and they could smell her as well as she could smell them. She decided if she were to make an attempt, it should be in the daytime and her pup should watch so that if she got one he would know it could be done.

She had not found any signs or smells of the wolf pack. Mother concluded it may be safer to bring the pup out than she had thought. She knew the cat was dead. She had followed it a couple nights after her female pup had died and found it dead near the river. She knew the little human was becoming a hunter too and was thankful he had defended her pups as best he could. He had strange habits like eating leaves, carving on sticks, and saving the skins of dead animals, but he was part of her pack now. She accepted him because he had accepted her. She wondered if he had the stamina for running a deer or elk. His sharpened stick could definitely kill. She headed home and caught a gopher pushing his fresh diggings up to the surface of his hole on the edge of the meadow.

Boy awoke with the idea he should sew a strap for his bag so he could sling it over his shoulder. The sun was rising when he crawled out from under the rock shelf. He saw his bag lying in the water and shook his head. That pup got into everything. He lifted the dripping bag from the water and laid it out in the morning sun to dry. It was softened up and collapsed on itself as it laid there. From the back of the cave Boy retrieved two more hides to cut into strips. He made the strips wider than the ones for string, wide enough for a shoulder strap the width of three of his fingers. He had to sew three strips together, end to end, to make the strap long enough. He overlapped the ends of each strip and punched the holes. He connected them with an in-and-out stitch he had watched Fire Woman use, keeping the hair sides matched up. Later he discovered the bag he'd left to dry in the sun was getting stiff again and this time in a wrinkled, collapsed position so the bag would be unusable. He took it back to the water pool and soaked it again. This time he worked the hide by stretching it in all directions just as he had seen Fire Woman soften a hide. Then he realized the wet hide could be turned inside out while it was soft. That would put the seams facing the inside. It worked perfectly! The seams were now inside with the hair on the outside. The bag looked better, and he wouldn't have to worry about hairs in his berries when it was time to pick them. He soaked the ends of his strap, then punched holes, and sewed the strap onto the bag. He had to figure out how to stretch the bag into the useable shape and let it dry. He solved that problem by stuffing the bag full of grass. Then he set it back out in the sun to dry.

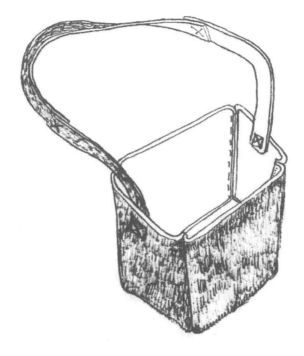

He went back to working on the fish spear, carving notches until he tired of it. This project would take some time. He walked up to the marmot holes to see if he could get another in his trap. He thought about how much time trapping took. Boy thought of all the things he could be doing rather than lying in wait for a marmot to come out of its hole. Several hours later, he returned with some fresh marmot meat he shared with Mother and the pup. He was pleased to discover that his bag was dry and in good shape.

Mother stayed in that night and all of them got a good night's rest. The next day the boy was going for another walk with his bag and spear. Mother took her pup out for another hunt. He decided to follow them at a distance and watch. They moved quickly and the boy had to jog along to keep them within sight. When Mother went into stalking mode, Boy stopped and took cover behind a larger tree. Pup watched too as she circled downwind of a brushy patch, her nose to the ground. Pup followed several wolf-lengths behind her. She burst into the brush and out ran two deer—a large one and a small one. She was hot on the tail of the small one, but the larger deer had turned and pursued her!

CHAPTER NINE

First Kill

The pup joined the chase, not realizing the danger the mother deer presented. The small deer circled in a wide path, coming directly at the boy. He instinctively readied his spear, but the deer passed so quickly he had no time to throw it. Pup was the next to pass. He had seen the arc of the circle the small deer was running in, and took a shortcut to head off the fawn. Mother was next. Although she was chasing the small deer, she was also aware of the large doe chasing her.

Immediately after Mother Wolf passed, the boy stepped out from behind the tree where he had been hiding. With his spear raised, he faced the doe head on. The doe was surprised to see a human. She panicked and spun in the opposite direction so quickly that Boy did not have time to throw his spear. He was disappointed in himself. Two deer had been close, but he hadn't been fast enough.

Mother Wolf now put on a burst of speed, cutting the circle as the pup had done and hitting the fawn broadside, knocking it to the ground. Pup was there in an instant and jumped on its back, biting it as hard as he could. Mother ripped a tendon from one of the fawn's legs. The deer managed to break away and was now off again running on three legs, with both wolves in pursuit.

Mother noticed Boy step out from behind the tree. She also realized the effect it had on the mother deer. The grown deer had circled back now, watching from a distance. She would fight a single wolf to the death but fighting a man was a different story. She knew men were much more dangerous. She saw the wolves knock down her fawn. She knew that it was now a decision of fighting for a wounded, if not dead, fawn or saving herself. The smell of blood was in the air, so the doe trotted off in the direction she knew other deer would be. There would be safety in numbers.

Mother now headed wide and turned the running fawn back toward the pup and the boy. The pup managed to knock the fawn over again but still didn't understand how to kill or disable it. He tried to grab the wounded leg because it was bloody, but he received a quick kick in the nose for his efforts. Mother caught up, ripped the second hind leg, and the fawn went down. The boy watched as the mother circled the fawn and watched the pup try to kill it. As the boy approached, Mother Wolf grabbed the fawn by the throat and jerked it down. But she let go and circled again. This time the young wolf understood and went for the deer's throat, cutting off the air supply to its lungs.

Catching up, the boy arrived and jabbed his spear through the deer's rib cage. The deer made a wheezing sound. It tried to kick with its last effort, then fell limp. Mother Wolf pranced around on her three good legs as if she was the best teacher ever. Both her students had helped not only in the hunt but also in the kill! She celebrated by ripping open the fawn's stomach and letting her students have first choice.

Boy had mixed emotions. He had just taken part in the savage ritual of hunter and prey. He was proud of the joint effort and the success of the kill, but he also felt sorry for the little deer. He did not find the innards all that appetizing, so he let the wolves eat their fill. While looking at the carcass as the wolves fed, he decided to salvage what he could of the hide. It might make a decent bag or a sleeping mat. With his knife he began skinning the deer, working from where Mother had ripped the stomach open, moving away from where the wolves were feeding. Ordinarily, being this close to a feeding wolf would have been very dangerous, but these three were now a pack, and Mother understood the boy. The boy understood her well enough to know she would let him have a share in a pack kill.

The wolves finished eating and wandered off to lie down. Mother thought the boy saved her a lot of work by removing the skin that she normally would have had to tear off. Boy cut off strips of meat and filled his bag. Rolling up the hide, he threw it over his shoulder. He could not pack all the meat, but he knew Mother and Pup would eat from it for several days. Then the other scavengers would clean up the rest. He headed for the cave. He was now carrying a heavy load and had to rest every so often. Mother had watched him load the meat. She knew what he would do with it and marveled at how handy it was to have the small man in her pack. He was always thinking ahead. She was still puzzled why he packed the hide back to the cave. She just accepted that as a quirk of this individual.

Pup was beside himself. He hadn't realized how thrilling a deer hunt could be. It seemed to be quite easy, and he wondered why they didn't hunt deer all the time. He was still unaware of the damage the doe could have done to him. His nose had a cut from the fawn's kick and was sore. He licked it over and over, but didn't let it bother him too much. He had now been part of a successful hunt and would never be the same again.

Boy knew this was the time to name the pup who had earned a name by participating in a kill. He was a warrior wolf now and needed a name. Boy looked at the pup, and the pup stared back, twisting his head to one side inquisitively. His ear showed the three distinct flaps the big cat had left him, and the pup's nose was red with swelling. Boy thought the pup looked funny for a young warrior. In fact, Pup looked like he was laughing at the whole situation.

"I name you 'Laughing Wolf,' the warrior and my brother," Boy said.

Pup ran to him and licked his face as if he understood what Boy had said and approved. Now it was the boy's turn to laugh.

Several days went by. Boy used the sun to dry most of the meat he had brought back. He stayed at the cave and worked on the fish spear. He carved all three jagged spear points while the spear shaft dried. He discovered that as one side dried faster than another, the wood bent toward the drier side. He began to rotate the shaft where it lay several times a day. He could test its straightness by looking down the shaft toward the light in the mouth of the cave. While slowly spinning the shaft in his fingers, he determined where a bend was forming. He bent the curves that formed back to a straight position, like it had been when he cut it green. At least once a day, he straightened the shaft like this. As the shaft's diameter shrank, the spear got lighter. By the time it was completely dry, it was stiff and straight and felt good in his hands. He tried laying the three jagged points up to the shaft on the narrow end. That made the points closer together than he remembered. He tried the larger diameter end of the shaft and that looked better. He tied on the three points with marmot hide cord as tight as he could, but they were unstable, so he carved three flat spots on the end of the thick end of the spear and carved a flat spot on each of the three points. It worked better but was still a bit loose. If he was lucky enough to jab a big fish, he didn't want to lose the fish and the points he had spent so much time working on.

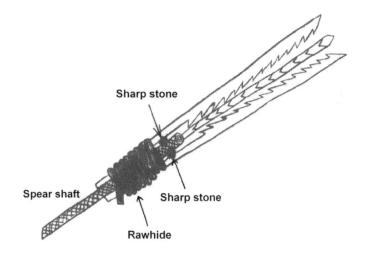

He took his spear to the river to test it. He looked for big fish, but finding none, he tried spearing a small one, but he kept missing. The fish were fast and he was always a bit above it. As the rawhide cord got wet, it became soft and loose, and the points started to fall out.

He sat down with the spear and thought, "What am I doing wrong?" He still didn't like the look of it. The spear he remembered the men using was splayed out so the tips branched kind of like a tree. His points were narrow and straight in line with the shaft. Sitting down on the river bank, he looked around and noticed lots of little rocks, some rounded and some sharp. He picked up a small, round pebble and laid it in between the shaft and one point. That caused the point to angle out away from the shaft as he remembered. But how would he make the point stay at that angle? It tended to slip out. He picked up a jagged stone about the same size and tried it. It stayed better. He found two more and set up all three points with jagged stones. Then he wrapped the points again with his wet cord. The cord stretched so that it was a bit tighter. The spear seemed to work better in the stream, but he still couldn't manage to stab a small fish. Giving up, he walked back to the cave. He hadn't realized it then, but he had solved both problems. When he returned to the spear a few days later, the rawhide cord had dried and shrunk. The force of the shrinking rawhide had crushed the rock into the wood of both the points and the shaft. Now the points were tight and could not shift their positions on the shaft either side to side or front to back. Boy was excited to try the spear again.

Then another thought occurred to him: Wouldn't the cord get wet again and come loose? He again set aside the fish spear for further thought.

Laughing Wolf now spent most of his time hunting. Boy no longer worried about having to feed the wolves. They even brought in a squirrel or gopher for him once in a while when they had killed more than they could eat. Laughing Wolf ran deer frequently, more frequently than Mother would have liked. He didn't always catch his prey, but he made sure they knew he was trying. When the wolves stayed out for three days, Boy was worried, but they returned to the cave as if they'd only been gone a short time.

Mother had taken Laughing Wolf to the valley and let him chase the pronghorn antelope. She figured the experience would do him good and he would quit harassing the main food source for a few days. Laughing Wolf had seen and experienced new things. Mother took him swimming across a slow-moving river. Laughing Wolf was not excited about getting in the water, but when Mother crossed the river, climbed the bank and kept going, he had to either do it or risk being left behind in a strange place. He plunged in, and to his surprise, found he could swim quite well. The cool water felt good. He shook off the weight of the water when he climbed out and ran to catch up with Mother. She had watched but pretended not to care when he caught up to her.

Down on the valley floor, she introduced him to the taste of raw eggs from a bird's nest on the ground in tall grass. Laughing Wolf chased a female pronghorn a short distance before she left him in her dust, wondering where she had disappeared to. Then he discovered rabbits. He spent hours in the brush along a stream until he finally caught one. He kept thinking that Boy needed to come along on the next trip because they would have so much fun together.

Boy had gone back to the site of the fawn kill when Mother and Laughing Wolf had not returned after the second night. Wandering through the area frequented by deer year round, he found several deer antlers shed that spring. They were still in good condition, smooth and hard. He remembered Fire Woman and the men had several tools made from the antlers of deer, so he gathered them in his bag. He still didn't know how to make a tool from antlers, but he had them ready if he ever figured out how to do it. He stored them in one of his hiding places in the back of the cave. Now the days were getting very hot and long. The boy thought about going for a swim, but wanted to wait at the cave in case the wolves returned.

The third day the wolves were gone was windy. Storm clouds were forming, but it was still very hot. It made Boy uneasy. He was quite worried but didn't go out on his own. He was relieved when both Mother and Laughing Wolf returned that evening. Laughing Wolf was obviously as happy as he was tired.

As nighttime fell, the thunder storm started. It didn't rain hard, just a token. Lightning strikes were hitting close, lighting up the cave. The crash of thunder was deafening, and Laughing Wolf paced back and forth, obviously uneasy. But Mother seemed calm. She had weathered storms before. From the protection of the cave, they all watched as the storm rolled through. Across the ravine the lightning flashes revealed long shadows of the forest but more devoid of color. Most flashes were from cloud to cloud, followed by loud rumbling, but once in a while, the bright flash hit the ground in the distance and nearly blinded them. It was quite a show, and better watched from the dryness of the cave. When the storm had passed, they finally fell asleep.

Boy woke to a smell he hadn't smelled in a while, and couldn't quite place. He got up and looked around, but saw nothing new in the cave. Mother was gone. Laughing Wolf was lethargic, still tired from his long trip. Mother came back into the cave and then turned and ran back out. It was a sign to follow her. He had watched her use it with the pup. Boy followed her, and Laughing Wolf was right behind him. As they crested the bench above the cave, Boy knew what he had smelled. It was fire!

CHAPTER TEN

Scout's Mystery

On the way back to the winter camp site, Wind's clan once again stopped to hunt deer. This was one of the best places they knew for deer hunting. It would be their last chance for a while to get some fresh hides to tan for clothes. Huckleberries were coming on as well. The sweet, little purple berries could be added to dried and shredded meat and then mixed with deer fat to make pemmican. This favorite food for traveling held a lot of energy for its weight, and kept well in a traveling pouch.

Wind in the Grass wanted to revisit the area of the massacre to see if the raiding party had returned to the battle site. He figured it was not that far out of the way, and he could look it over and be back near the clan before dark. He worked his way quietly toward the meadow above the cave. Walking among the trees, he heard movement ahead and took cover to make sure he was not seen. Then he witnessed something so unusual he couldn't believe his eyes.

He spotted two wolves out hunting. One older female was running on three legs. One of the rear legs had been wounded and had healed up unusable. The other was a nearly grown male pup with a ripped-up ear. They were traveling together. Following them was a small boy, maybe nine or ten winters old, naked except for a ragged loin cloth and carrying a short spear like the men who had been killed that spring. The boy also carried a rough-sewn carry bag that seemed pretty light. He was jogging at a distance behind the wolves. At first Wind thought maybe the boy was hunting the wolves, but they were very much aware of him and seemed even to be traveling slower to accommodate his short legs. Then it happened. The female wolf flushed a fawn from a thicket. She immediately began chasing the fawn, but at the same time, the fawn's mother pursued her. The young male wolf caught onto the game and joined in the running of the small deer. By this time, the boy was close enough to have walked right into the hunt! The fawn had circled and run right past the boy, who had stepped beside a large tree. He had raised his short spear and stepped into the oncoming doe's path. He didn't throw his spear, but managed to turn the doe away from the wolves! The injured female hamstrung the fawn shortly thereafter, but was obviously teaching the younger wolf how to kill a larger prey animal. She purposefully had shown it how to grab the throat of the fawn once it was down, but then she backed off to let the male take hold. The boy had come running up just at this time and ran his spear through the fawn. They had all taken meat from the fawn and the boy took the hide as well. He was using a knapped blade for a knife. It seemed more advanced than the rest of his tools.

Wind in the Grass was utterly amazed. What could all this mean? Did the boy domesticate the wolves? Where were the boy's people? His clothes showed no sign of tribal customs and his hair was unkempt, not styled in any tribal manner. Were they enemies or was he a member of the people who had been attacked last spring? There were so many questions to be answered. Wind in the Grass wanted to stay and follow the three hunt mates, but he knew he did not have the time. He was needed back protecting his own clan. He decided to return to his duties. He would not yet tell anyone what he had seen. This was a mystery to be pondered for a while. Some would take it as a bad omen and would want to move on. Wind did not see this as a threat to his people. They needed their deer hunting and berry gathering time. The enemy was not here. If they were, the boy and wolves would not have been hunting in the open.

Wind couldn't let this mystery go. He needed answers. He returned and told the elders of other news but kept for himself what he had seen of the boy. He asked the elders to relieve him of duties for a time so he could pursue a mystery he wanted to understand. He was old enough to command the respect of the elders. He was fast becoming an elder himself. A replacement was chosen to perform Wind's duties. This was a chance for a younger scout to prove himself. The elders had honored the old scout as well as the younger one. It was a good decision. Wind was asked to inform the elders of his status before they left for the winter camps. He agreed.

Wind took his survival kit with him and a cloak that doubled as a sleeping blanket or coat. In this he rolled up his necessities: fire tinder of fine, dried grasses and rotten crumbling wood which must be kept dry; a small bag of dried meat, although mostly, he ate off the land as he traveled; for repairing his leather goods, a sewing kit consisting of dried and pounded sinew, a bone awl and bone needle, all wrapped in a lightweight cloth of brain-tanned deer hide that could be used as a patch if needed; his bow and arrows for dealing with an enemy, although he tried to avoid conflict when out on his own. Most of the time, his bow was not needed. When he did have to fight the enemy, it was usually at close range so that the fight was hand to hand.

Wind in the Grass found the fawn carcass where it had been killed. He followed the boy's footprints, tracking him to the cave. He watched for many days as the boy went about his business. He watched as the boy lay for hours with string in hand to trap a marmot. He watched as the boy emerged from the cave with a fishing spear and managed to catch a fish. He was amazed. There was no sign of other people. The boy was living off what he killed or gathered. There might be another person in the cave, but if there was, they were too old or wounded to come outside. The wolves came and went from the cave. They were difficult to avoid. "Wind" suspected the female knew he was watching, and that she did not appreciate his presence in their territory. Wind kept his distance enough not to alarm her too much. This distance made it hard to get a vantage point to see into the cave. Wind would have to wait to know if the boy was truly alone with the wolves. He knew the boy had seen survival skills in action, but had not been taught all he needed.

Although the boy was sufficient in his skills to feed himself, Wind noticed many simple improvements he could teach the boy to make his life better. The wolves had made the boy's life easier. They had hunting capabilities way beyond that of the boy's and shared their kills with him. How could this be? How could a boy who would usually be just another meal to wolves the size of these two, be living, even sharing with them? He could have been abandoned as a very young boy and the female wolf had adopted him. But if that were the case, how did he come by the loin cloth? The carry bag? No, he had been with people of some sort. But who? No adult clansman would have let the boy befriend two wolves. Was he driven out of a tribe because of his friendship with the wolves? That seemed unlikely. A boy that young would not be able to spend enough time with wild wolves to become their friend if he lived with other adults. Wolves would be a danger to human young and their pack animals.

The boy looked wild himself. His carry bag and weapons were very effective but simply made. No grandmother had taught him the fine sewing to make a shirt and leggings. The boy's specific clothing would have placed him as a member of a familiar clan. The boy's spear was like that of the men who had been killed. Did he belong to them, or had the boy found the spear? The boy was living in the cave now, a cave that had been occupied last spring by those same men with primitive weapons. They were most likely the people who had influenced this boy's life. Did these people keep wolves? Wind did not think so. If they had, the wolves would have been part of the massacre he had found last spring. Wolves are fiercely protective of their pack. If they had been in the cave protecting the boy, he would have had encountered them.

Perhaps the boy did survive the massacre and somehow befriended the wolves. This was the most bewildering mystery Wind had ever encountered. There had to be spirits involved.

The relationship between the boy and wolves was too much for Wind to ignore. He had to find out how this came about and whether spirits, good or evil, were involved. The only way he would know for sure was to try to communicate with the boy. But how? More than likely, they did not speak the same language. He would have to ease himself into the boy's life. He didn't want to scare the boy away from his cave or even take him away from his wolf family, but he felt a burning desire to learn the boy's story. He knew he could teach the boy other skills to improve his survival abilities, but would his contact actually improve the boy's life?

Wind in the Grass was older than most active scouts. He had never had a family of his own, and would soon be turning his scouting responsibilities over to the younger scouts. He fancied himself becoming a member of the "Big Bellies," a group of elders highly respected for their wisdom and experience in concerns of the people. Of course, he would have to be asked by a current Big Bellies member and officially accept the role before his people would accept him in that role. Such an honor would be announced to all, and the clan would have a large celebration. More attention than he liked, yet in a way, he still longed to be part of that group. He would be respected for his knowledge and would help to train the boys who wanted to become a tribal scout.

Wind moved into the marmot colony on a day when the boy was down by the creek and the wolves had gone hunting. He set up a dead fall trap on a marmot trail that was not being used. The trap was very similar to the one the boy had been using, except that the marmot would trigger this trap on its own, so the boy would not have to wait to pull a string.

This trap used a leaning flat rock for a weight and a short stout stick for a supporting post like the boy's stick and string trap, but Wind in the Grass had made it more complicated. Instead of supporting the leaning rock, the post supported a lever stick. The short end of the lever stick supported the leaning deadfall rock. The other, lower end of the lever had a short string tied to it that stretched parallel with the ground back to and around the post's base. The other end of this string had a small trigger stick tied slightly off center. This small stick had the short end pulled against the post and the longer end braced against a bait stick that held the whole thing from falling. His bait stick was a long, thin piece of wood that reached from the post to the base of the leaning rock. It had animal fat melted on the end that was furthest under the dead fall rock. When the trap was set, the weight of the flat dead fall rock leaning on the lever stick kept down pressure on the lever. In turn, the other end of the lever stick kept outward pressure on the string. The string, pulling on the small stick, put pressure both on the base of the post and on the bait-stick that was lodged against the underside of the deadfall rock just above where it met the ground. If a marmot was attracted to the smell of the fat, and chewed or even bumped the bait stick, the whole thing would crush the marmot under the dead fall rock.

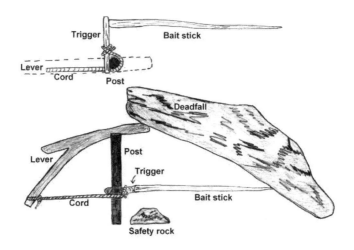

Wind left the trap for the boy to find. It was set away from the active trails so that it would not likely be set off. He covered it with small pieces of dirt and leaves from the surrounding ground to make it appear to have been there for a long time. He hoped the boy would think it had been set long before and would not jump to the conclusion that his enemy had returned. Wind then melted into the background, lingering to watch the boy's reaction.

It took most of a week for the boy to find the set trap. He immediately understood its purpose and studied it intently. He kept looking around and appeared nervous. He took a stick and triggered the trap. He gathered up the parts, including the flat rock, and took it to his cave to examine closer. Wind in the Grass did not see the boy for some time. Several days later, he noticed the trap was reset on an active marmot trail. He was satisfied that he had helped the boy, but he was not done yet. He was contemplating the next thing he could do for the boy without revealing himself when an unexpected sound caught his attention. Human voices! Enemy voices! Wind in the Grass quietly investigated. It was a group of three warriors who were traveling toward the campground of Wind's people. Their path would bring them right in front of the cave entrance. He knew that if they found the boy alone, they would capture or kill him.

CHAPTER ELEVEN

Fire!

The lightning had hit a pine tree, and it was burning around the base. Although the fire was small, it had the potential to start a range or forest fire. The tree had stood out alone. There was not much more around the base of it except short grass and the dead, dry limbs that the snows from past winters had forced the tree to drop. Still, dry grass can carry a fire to the next tree. Boy could see the worry in Mother's eyes. She didn't know what to do. She thought of fire as an enemy and figured the human might help.

Boy had a different idea. He gathered wood and fed the fire! He stamped out fire in the grass around the tree while gathering the larger burning sticks into one pile. When he finished, the fire had gone out on three sides and was well contained on the fourth. Luck had kept the whole tree from going up in flames. It had a spiral scar from the top to the ground that had split the bark open. Eventually, the tree would die, but it had been saved from the fire by Boy.

Mother watched as Boy found more wood and set it to the flame. When he had several sticks burning together, he carefully carried them to the cave, and put them in the old fire pit. Then he returned for more. After three trips, he had enough coals to keep the cave fire burning while he gathered more wood. He deprived the fire at the tree base of fuel to the point he could stamp it out. Once that was done, he started gathering wood for his cave fire. He worked all day long gathering wood even though the day was hot enough he really didn't need the heat. But boy knew how valuable fire was. His people could make fire when they needed it with certain woods, spinning one piece like a drill on the other. He remembered watching Fire Woman do it very quickly. He had been in charge of not letting the fire go out once she had started it. He did not know how to start a fire, but he could keep it going. This was common practice in a long-term camp, and he had kept the fire going all winter.

Mother left for the day, worried about this fire the boy was playing with but not wanting to be too near it. Laughing Wolf had followed as he had seen enough fire for today and Mother always was doing something fun.

As night fell, Boy brought in a large stack of firewood and set up some quickly made drying racks for meat. He cooked a slice or two and ate it warm. It was a good feeling. He was really pleased with his gift of fire.

The wolves returned, more to check on their pack mate than to come near the fire. The fire didn't seem to bother Laughing Wolf. It was new to him, but Boy seemed to know how to handle it. Besides, as the night cooled, the heat from the fire felt good. But Mother paced. She laid down away from the heat of the fire.

Fire Woman had taught Boy how to blow a coal into fire, how to preserve a coal by burying a chunk of rotted wood with hot coals under dirt for a day. With no air, there would be no flames and no flame made the coal last longer. Fire Woman had also taught him how to wrap a coal tightly with rotting wood inside green grass and larger leaves so it could be carried as the tribe moved and then re-blown into a fire when camp was made. He spent the night thinking of what he could do now that he had a fire.

Berries were ripening quickly. Small, purple berries appeared all over the hillsides. It gave Boy a thrill to gather them and then eat a handful. The wolves ate a few too, but they didn't have the patience to pick them off the bushes like Boy did. Boy was drying berries in the sun. He started using the third pit in the cave to store his growing supply of food. He made rawhide bags to store the dried berries, then stacked the bags in the grandfathers' bin, and covered them with the flat stone lid.

The nights were turning cooler even if the days weren't. The fall colors were coming on, and Boy's instinct told him winter was closely behind. He had better be ready.

Mother and Laughing Wolf had hunted deer again, taking a full-grown doe. They had singled her out, the weakest of the herd. Mother had led the boy to their kill. She wanted him to have a share before other scavengers got to it. Boy quickly skinned the hide and stripped meat from the haunch to fill his carrying bag. He hauled the meat and hide to the cave in two trips. Now that he had fire, he could dry meat much faster, so he salvaged as much as he could. Some fat and meat clung to the hide. He knew he had to clean the hide before it turned rancid and made the cave stink. Sitting outside the mouth of the cave, he scraped the hide clean. His hands were getting so greasy it was hard to hold the scraping stone. When he went down to the creek to wash his hands, he realized that water alone wasn't working. The fat from the hide repelled the water so it was not washing off. He grabbed a handful of fine sand from the creek bottom to scrub off the greasy film. The sand scraped through the grease and carried it off his skin. He cleaned his hands as well as he could, then he went back to scraping the hide.

He was thinking again about what had to be done to prepare for winter. He would like to catch some fish. The men had caught fish in the river, and Fire Woman had dried them in the smoke of the fire. Now that he had a fire, he could do that. He just needed to complete the fish spear and find some bigger fish. He remembered the crayfish and realized he could even cook that now. He returned to the cave and checked the fire.

Now that Boy had to maintain the fire, his daily duties changed. He spent a lot of time gathering wood. He needed more and larger pieces to burn at night so he could sleep and still have coals in the morning. He also needed to be able to leave for a day and come back to hot coals. He stacked the wood next to the fire, and the pile grew, taking up a large portion of the front of the cave. He set a log so the fire would burn the end of it and figured it should last for several hours. He grabbed his short spear and long fishing spear and headed out. Stopping to stretch out the doe hide, he put rocks along the edges to keep it flat as it dried, just as he had with the marmot hides. He realized the rocks would not hold the big hide, so he quickly made some pegs from the limbs of the firewood. He used a rock to hammer the pegs through the rawhide and into the ground to keep it stretched out as much as he could as it dried.

When he finished, he scooped the fat he had scraped off the hide, planning to move it away from the cave so when it went rancid the smell would not attract larger predators to the cave, not to mention the meat-thieving birds. He carried the fat down the slope and dumped it in a place where, from the mouth of the cave, he could watch what animals it attracted. His hands were greasy again from handling the fat. On the way back to the cave, it occurred to him that if he were to rub the greasy fat into the rawhide lashing on the fish spear, it might keep the water from soaking into the lashing and loosening the binding. He grabbed his fish spear and traveling gear and headed back down the slope. Stopping at the bush where he had tossed the deer fat, he spread some fat on the joint and rubbed it all over the rawhide. Once he had covered it, he washed his hands with sand to remove the slick fat from his fingers. He headed for the creek to test his fish spear. The spear held tight to its points. Now he was ready for fishing!

He walked down the river looking for bigger fish. After a while, he found a pool with bigger fish in the bottom, but the pool was too big and deep for him to use the spear. Boy kept walking and found a smaller hole with at least one big fish. He tried jabbing the fish, but missed. The fish swam around the hole looking to escape, but had no hiding place, so it settled back into the bottom. Boy tried and missed again. Pulling the spear up closer to the surface, he noticed it looked bent, but he pulled the spear all the way out of the water, and it was straight. He stuck the spear into the water again, and it looked bent right where it went underneath the water. He pushed the spear in deep, and the bend in the shaft moved up the handle, always staying where the spear met the water. Boy figured water must make things look like they are in a different spot than they actually are. Since the spear looked like it bent upward, the fish must look higher in the water than it really was. He decided to aim lower than the fish next time. He moved the spear point closer to the fish, then aimed lower and jabbed. He wasn't ready for the battle he fought when the spear connected with the fish. He almost lost hold of the handle. The fish was wiggling intensely, and he had to work hard to direct it to shore while not falling in himself! He finally worked the fish to shore and hauled his fish up on land. It was a good-sized fish, still not as big as the fish the men used to bring back. He wondered why he couldn't find a fish that big. He looked for more fish but did not find any big enough to try to spear. He stopped to clean the guts from his fish, washing it in the stream before heading back to the cave.

Boy got the fire going again, and rounded up a short stick. He sharpened it and ran it through the fish's mouth down into the tail meat. Then put a little stick sideways to hold open the sides of the fish. He propped the fish over the fire and let it cook slowly.

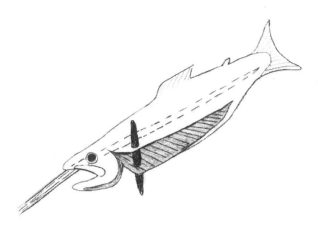

After all those days of marmot meat and even with the deer meat, the fish tasted so wonderful, and it was cooked! A hot meal warmed him inside. It was a good feeling.

CHAPTER TWELVE

The Enemy

Wind in the Grass recognized the three men were of the same tribe as the raiding party last spring. He had to do something. He let himself be seen. He was pretending to gather edible roots on a hillside. The three warriors split up and began an attack. Wind walked around a large rose bush as calmly as if he was gathering firewood or medicinal plants. One of the warriors snuck up quickly behind, but as he tried to move into an attack position, he discovered his target had vanished. Looking around, he caught a glimpse of the older man further up the hill rounding the next bush. Wind kept his pursuers going in this manner until he had led them farther away from the cave, moving to the northwest.

The warriors were growing tired of this game. When one had a long shot with his bow and arrow, he took it. The stone-tipped arrow sank into Wind's calf muscle on his right leg. He was sent sprawling. He quickly broke off the shaft just outside his skin, concealed the arrow shaft so the warrior would not find it, and disappeared into the bushes.

The game had just changed for Wind, from harassing the enemy to a life-or-death trial. The warrior moved in to investigate, but not finding a dead man, his arrow, or a blood trail, he was confused. One of his friends gave him a hard time about missing his shot. He kept looking for his arrow or signs that he had actually hit his target. The other two men went ahead of him and split up.

By this time, Wind had started bleeding, not a lot but enough to drip on the ground giving the enemy knowledge that they had wounded him and indicating which direction he was traveling. Wind doubled back on his own tracks to leave two separate blood trails and confuse his pursuers. The warriors hollered when they found blood. One warrior split off on the right-branching trail, the other two followed the left branch. Wind took the time to stop the bleeding as best he could. He broke the arrow shaft off outside of his wound, then cut a strip of leather from his robe and picked some low grow-ing leaves that had medicinal value. He packed the wound and tied the leather strip around his leg to hold it in place. He slid the arrow shaft under a bush so the enemy trackers would not find it. He had his survival gear rolled up in his robe and slung over his back, but had no time to remove the arrowhead from the wound just yet. He would rid himself of the enemy, then remove the rest of the arrow from his leg. He doubled back around again coming in behind the lone war-rior. Being a scout and responsible for protecting his clan from all en-emies, he knew what he had to do. He did the grisly job so quickly the warrior never knew he was there. He left the body at the end of the blood trail and moved on, leaving a very easy trail to follow. He wanted the other warriors to follow him to his next ambush.

The two warriors, having followed their blood trail to its end, hurried back to track the other trail, afraid that their accomplice would get all the glory. They found him in a pool of his own blood. This not only scared them, but made them even angrier. Finding Wind's deliberate trail, they began following it again. This time they were aware of how crafty the man they hunted really was.

Wind pulled his warrior hand axe from his belt. He circled his pursuers once again, never letting them see him, but not getting so far away he couldn't tell exactly where they were. As the two warri-ors passed, he threw the axe at the head of the second one. The war-rior had seen the motion out of the corner of his eye and ducked. The blade caught his shoulder and sliced through the muscle just enough to bleed and hurt badly. The hand axe had done some damage but flew on past. The warrior screamed his rage and ran at Wind in the Grass. Wind deftly moved out of the way, and with a hard stroke to his back, sent him flying into the thorns of a wild rose bush. Another arrow just missed Wind's head as he dove for cover. Keeping to the low brush, he moved past the enemy once again, picking up his axe and moving on. Neither the axe nor the rose bush had wounded the warrior badly, but the wounds to the warrior's pride cut very deep. He was going to kill this enemy and claim his hair!

The two warriors remaining took this personal war more seriously now, splitting up to track and cover each other's advances. The one with a wounded shoulder had been the one who originally hit Wind with an arrow. He was game for another long shot. Wind in the Grass heard it coming and twisted down and away from the oncoming arrow, but it was too late. The arrow pierced his left side just above his waist, causing a flesh wound through the roll of flabby skin a man his age tends to get regardless of whether he is an expert scout or not. He broke the protruding point off the shaft and pulled the arrow from the wound the way it had entered. It hurt and bled some. Wind figured it was time to end this war. He was approaching the river. He was nearing a river and could hear rushing water. The two warriors were gaining on him. He figured the sound would help disguise his movements and he could get another opportunity to take one out. Unfortunately, he didn't get the chance.

As he rounded a large boulder and ducked another arrow, he came face to face with a large brown-colored bear. But it wasn't just any bear. This bear's face had many battle scars. It had tasted man before.

Last spring, this bear had fought off a pack of wolves to claim his prize. He was in the mood for more fresh meat and some had just come within his grasp.

The bear was completely aware of, and drawn to the smell of blood dripping from Wind's wounds. Landing a blow on Wind's left shoulder, the bear sent him to the ground, immediately clamped down on Wind's wounded leg, and began shaking him. Wind felt his lower leg snap in two like a twig.

All those years of scouting taught Wind to enter a calm state of mind when fear overtook him. He was thinking how the bear had gone into battle without making much sound. The bear's reaction to him was not so much being startled as it was calculating and evil in nature.

The bear flipped him forward and tried to pin him with one of his great front paws. Wind slammed down his hand axe with such force that it cut two toes off the bear's front left paw.

Screaming its rage, the bear dropped Wind in a heap. It rose up on its hind legs, intending to bring its massive weight down on Wind's crumpled body. Just as the bear stood its full height, the two warriors rounded the boulder, surprising the bear as much as themselves. Their sudden arrival drew the bear's attention away from Wind. It twisted toward the new threat. Both warriors launched their arrows into the bear, but neither arrow hit where it should have. They had cut no more than flesh wounds in the giant predator. Already standing, the bear struck out with a giant paw, crushing one warrior's skull against the rocks.

Wind in the Grass rolled out from under the bear and under a downed tree. The second warrior had turned to run, but the bear was already moving toward him as he sprinted back into the brush. The bear took three bounds and was on top of him. Wind heard screaming as he stuffed his hand axe and the two bear claws into the end of his rolled cloak and dragged himself to the river. He didn't want to be there when the bear returned. Lifting his rolled cloak as best he could, he slid into the water and let the current carry him downstream.

CHAPTER THIRTEEN

Mother's Concern

Boy left on his rounds, heading up to the marmot colony. He was setting up the usual dead fall trap and stretched the string back to a bush he could lay down and hide behind. He had just got comfortable and was looking around when he noticed another trap, one he hadn't seen before. The trap had been left set. At first glance, it appeared to have been there for some time. It was set on an old unused marmot trail not likely to be triggered. Boy could see the ingenious design allowed the hunter to leave while the marmot triggered the trap on its own. Examining it closely, Boy reached out with a stick and triggered the set. It collapsed perfectly. Looking around, he saw no one. He checked for footprints around the set, but saw no sign of recent human activity. Still, it did not seem right that he had been trapping this area, but hadn't noticed it before. He gathered up the pieces and looked at each one to see how it was constructed. It looked to him as if the sticks had been cut recently. He felt as if someone was watching him. He looked carefully, but still could not see anyone. He gathered the trap pieces and his own stick and string and returned to the safety of the cave to study it more, and to practice setting the trap. Had the enemy set a trap not knowing he was there? He would wait it out a while returning. He had enough meat for now.

Mother Wolf and the pup were ranging further from the cave. The pup was learning what he needed to survive on his own. They returned to the cave for a night, and then were out for two or three nights. Boy figured the fire in the cave may have something to do with Mother's movements. She was never comfortable around the fire. Laughing Wolf was OK with the fire but was much more interested in his mother's teachings than playing with Boy.

The boy found himself lonely when the wolves were away for several days. Mother was as fully healed as she ever would be. He could not keep up with her unless she slowed to allow him to follow. Sometimes in the evenings, he heard them howling in the distance. He also heard other wolves answer them. He wondered what they were saying.

After a couple days, the boy's fears had subsided. He returned to the marmot colony to set the trap he had found, along with a duplicate he had made using the first as a pattern. He picked an active trail to set the first trap. He had rubbed animal fat on the bait sticks to make it smell like food, knowing that all small animals craved fat. Using a safety rock to keep from catching himself, he set the trap as he had practiced. He gently removed the safety rock, and then went to set the second trap further down the ridge. He returned to the spot where he had found the trap set. He found no human tracks except his own. He was very aware of any possible danger, but saw nothing disturbing. He figured the trap must really have been there from before. Maybe Talking Elk had left it. He decided to see what the river had to offer today. This time he didn't need to stay and pull the trap string.

Laughing Wolf was a bundle of energy. He had grown during the summer and was constantly exploring. Mother had taken him out and hunted all sorts of animals. He was becoming a proficient hunter, feeding himself quite well on mice and other rodents of the meadow. Mother howled with him and their singing elicited return songs from other roaming wolves. This excited the pup even more, but Mother would not allow the other wolves to find them. She knew she must allow Laughing Wolf to gain his full strength before he was subjected to the rigors of pack hierarchy. She wanted him to be leader material when they returned to her pack, if they ever did.

Mother had led Laughing Wolf north to follow the river upstream to see what they could find. It was more of a lesson on the boundary of the pack's territory than a hunt. Laughing Wolf took advantage of a chance to chase a weasel hunting along the creek bank. The weasel proved to be quicker and a bit trickier than the pup had predicted. The little brown hunter with a yellow belly doubled back on its path and climbed a tree where he watched as the pup searched the underbrush for him.

Mother was aware of the weasel's position but had no interest in the little hunter. She was sitting further up the bank when she caught the scent of a human, and it was not the boy! She woofed a warning to the pup who quickly fell in behind her. They moved in the direction of the smell, inland to where she found a blood trail and began following it. It was human blood but she wanted to know just how many were about. She was extremely cautious not to show herself.

Laughing Wolf understood her actions and concealed his movements in the shadows, keeping slightly back but always knowing where Mother was by her scent. Mother found the first dead warrior and moved on, figuring that one posed no threat now. The trail continued, and she followed it for quite some time. The men had covered a lot of ground at a fast pace. Suddenly a familiar smell filled her keen nose. The bear! The same old grizzled male she had once fought had been here, and the humans had crossed its path. She suspected what she would find, but curiosity drove her forward.

The fight was over, but the bear might still be a threat. Mother found another dead human by the rock and the remains of a half-eaten one had been partially buried under a downed tree, then covered with debris.

Turning and leaving quickly, Mother was not completely satisfied. The moisture in the air near the river had a tendency to trap smells and send them downstream with the movement of air above the rushing water. She could be missing something. She followed the river a short distance. Sure enough, there was more scent on the wind. Mother followed the riverbank downstream, making sure to stay in the shadows. Soon the wolves found themselves peering through the undergrowth at a single human sitting near a small fire. He was alive, but not moving much.

Mother knew it was not good practice to get close to humans. Good to know where they were, how many they were, and then to avoid them. She knew now that the human threat consisted only of the one man, but the bear was near and might pose a bigger threat if she and her pup had to fight it. The wolves lingered only briefly before returning to the cave and checking on the boy.

The next day Mother led both the boy and the pup south. Boy knew Mother was trying to tell him something. She was acting quite concerned with him, staring him directly in his face. Boy checked his traps on the way. They had not been disturbed yet. He left them and continued following Mother.

When they passed by the site of their first pack kill, Boy inspected what remained of the small deer's skeleton. It was mostly cleaned off by the insects of the forest. He admired the bones and though he knew tools could be made with them, he was unsure what he could make. He didn't have the time now so he left them lay and followed Mother. They found little in the way of hunting, but Boy found another large patch of berries, which he gladly ate and put some in his carry bag for later. Also, he found a rather large deer antler that had been shed that spring.

Deer drop their antlers every spring, as do elk. Then they grow new ones to fight with by the coming fall. The bone material that antlers were grown from provided the small creatures of the forest with a source of calcium, and this antler had small teeth marks from a field mouse. The shed antlers could also provide a hard material to make tools. He decided to take this one with him. It was rather pretty, he thought, in the way it had been polished brown with white tips. It fit awkwardly in his bag, but was secure enough to make the trip.

It was dark by the time they returned. The fire still smoldered. Boy had left it buried so that he could restart it. He quickly added some tinder and gently blew it into flame. Then he added more wood to gradually make it bigger until his fire was sufficient.

Mother moved to lie down outside the mouth of the cave. Laughing Wolf lay with Boy on top of the sleeping shelf. Boy, too, had grown and although he could still fit under the shelf it was not as comfortable as it had been. Instead, he slept in his fur robe on top of the shelf with his best friend and his spear close by.

The next day when Boy checked the traps, one had caught a marmot! This was a very good thing. It now freed up Boys' time to gather other food. He reset the trap and moved on.

As the days went on, Boy kept himself busy preparing for winter. He dragged small logs back to the cave to use as firewood. He stacked at the entrance to the cave to block the coming winter wind. He didn't know how much wood he would need, but he knew he would need a lot. He gathered and hauled it from as far away as he could, figuring that if he needed more in the winter, it would be best to leave the closer wood to gather when the snow kept him from traveling very far.

CHAPTER FOURTEEN

A Long Night

Wind in the Grass had a rough ride downstream. Although the cold of the water shrunk his blood vessels and slowed his bleeding, the river was far from a smooth flow, and with only one leg to work with, he bounced against a few rocks. He made it through a set of rapids by keeping his head above water and his feet downstream. When he finally reached a slower-moving pool, he let the circulating currents bring him close to shore. He pulled himself up onto the bank, still gripping his survival gear, which was no longer dry. Exhausted and in pain, he lay down on the rock and soon lost consciousness.

Sometime later, Wind awoke and pulled himself up to a sitting position to check his injuries. His side wound was deep, but not life threatening. He removed his legging on the wounded leg. It was not a pretty sight. Wind in the Grass took stock of his supplies. His knife was at his side still in one piece. His bow and a few arrows had been inside the rolled bundle. The arrows were OK, but the bow had been broken into two pieces. It was not going to fling any more arrows, but it might still have a use. The cloak that he used as a sleeping blanket, or a jacket, was soaking wet. His tool kit was still intact. And of course, he had the hand axe and two bear claws. His wet fire tinder was useless. He had no dried meat left. He had used it while watching the boy, not wanting to take the time to find other food sources. He had figured he could always get more meat later. It may have been a mistake, but he had more immediate problems than hunger.

It was his knife, the sinew, and bone needle he was most interested in now. Wind straightened out his leg. It had been broken in two places and the arrow tip was still embedded. He had used his hands to bend his lower leg back at the knee so he could see the arrow wound. With his knife he cut open the wound on each side of the arrowhead, so he could see into the wound to determine the direction in which the stone point stuck in his leg. Surprisingly, cutting the wound bigger didn't hurt as much as he had imagined it would. His body was still in shock from the multiple fractures imposed by the bear. The tip was embedded in the bone but not too deep. He worked it back and forth in the direction of the cutting edges. He winced. This part hurt badly! He would have to make the hole in his bone bigger to allow him to work the tip loose. If he had tried to move the obsidian arrowhead side to side rather than with the sharp edges, it would have broken off inside the wound and might never have been removed.

Once the point was out, he allowed the wound to bleed a bit to clean it. Separating the strands of his strip of sinew, he pulled a fine thread loose, and put the end through the eye of his needle. He knew from experience that poking the needle up through his skin from inside the edge of a wound hurt less and would cause less damage than trying to force the needle down through his skin from the outside. He rubbed the tip of the needle on a rough rock to sharpen it. Stitching the wound closed with the sinew thread, he tied off the ends. The wound still bled, but he knew it would stop now that the wound was held shut with the sinew.

He checked his side wound again. It needed only a few stitches to close it. Although the bleeding had been slowed by the cold water, it started again when he began stitching. It would stop once the stitches were in place.

Now came the hard part. Even as brave as Wind was, he feared the pain of setting a bone. He wasn't sure he could do it. He would need a few things first. He took three arrows, broke off their sharp tips and stripped them of their feathers. He aligned the arrow shafts next to his leg, and trimmed them to the right length. He did this by scoring the shaft, cutting deep into the arrow wood with his knife as he turned the arrow on the knife's blade. He then snapped the shaft off at the score line. Readying cordage, he went to work on his leg. Feeling through the torn muscle, the puncture wounds from the bear's teeth, he could tell his leg was broken in two places and his knee was dislocated. With great effort, he pulled his lower leg straight, and snapped his knee back into place. It was so painful he passed out again in the process. Once his knee was back in place, he started aligning the bones. By lodging his foot between two larger rocks on the riverbank and pulling against it, he made the largest bone align itself with the other end of the break. He then lined up the next fragment of bone that was below the knee and aligned the break. From where he sat, his leg looked pretty straight. He slid one arrow shaft behind his leg to support his knee, and then lined up the other arrows on each side of his leg. He started wrapping the cordage around the leg, tying the arrow shafts in place. Once he had immobilized his right leg, he worked the legging back over it for more protection.

With his wounds attended to, he turned his attention to what he would need to survive the night. He had water handy at the river, but now needed shelter, protection from predators and the elements. He wrapped up his equipment in the robe again, then dragged himself to the river bank and drank deeply. He knew he couldn't allow himself to get dehydrated, but he had to get back up off the river bank to find shelter from the cool night to prevent this body from getting too cold.

His elders had taught him as a small child the dangers of letting his body temperature drop too low. Once when his clan's enemies had left a warrior naked in the snow to die, he had witnessed the madness it could cause. Wind in the Grass had found the man and tried to move him into a snow cave and build a fire to warm him. Completely unaware of the cold, the man danced in the snow on his frostbitten feet. His ears and nose were white! He would not listen to the young scout and died shortly thereafter from exposure. That is when Wind promised himself to never be taken by this madness.

Crawling to a large rock, Wind managed to stand up on his good leg, but it was no use. He could not put pressure on the broken leg.

He would have to crawl. Lowering himself to the ground, he crawled away from the creek's rocky shoreline. The creek was lined with a cottonwood grove, so Wind in the Grass gathered a couple of straight pieces of cottonwood limbs as he crawled. The crawling took more out of him than he had realized. When he found his way blocked by a large boulder on one side and a group of fallen cottonwood trees in front, he decided to stay and make that his shelter. He figured the boulder would reflect heat from a fire, if he could get one started, and the logs would deflect any cold air that might blow in. Looking around, he found a rotten log, crawled to it and gathered a couple handfuls of the finest rotted wood. It was decomposed enough that he ripped it out with his hands and crumbled it up to a grainy powder. Now he needed some dry grass, leaves, or moss. The cottonwood had dropped a lot of leaves over the years, so he gathered the driest ones he could find. They weren't holding together well, so he pulled some tall, dry grasses and wrapped them around themselves into a bowl shape. Stuffing the grass with the dried cottonwood leaves, he made a nest, crumbled the bits of rotten wood into this nest, and set it down in front of the boulder. Then he gathered as much firewood as he could—from pieces as small as his bone awl to the heaviest branches he could grab without hurting his leg. The fallen cottonwood trees provided almost everything he needed to get a fire going.

He built a tipi of small sticks leaving one side open to set the nest in. The tipi shape allowed air to get between the sticks to encourage flame upwards catching the wood on fire.

Coal

Rotten wood

Nest of dry grass or moss

Once he had prepped for starting the fire, he needed to make the coal. He took out his broken bow limb and hacked off the handle with his hand axe. Wind then thinned the limb until it could bend easily in his hand, like a miniature bow. He loosely tied his bowstring on the reshaped mini bow. He split the straight piece of cottonwood limb, set down half, and split the other half again. He used his hand axe to rough out a straight drill spindle, rounding the edges as he went. Then he split the remaining cottonwood half again, cutting off the outside rounded part to make a small piece that was flat on both sides for a fire board. He used his knife to drill the start of a hole in the fire board near the edge. Now he just needed a socket. He looked around for a rock with a hole in it, but to no avail. Finally he decided he would have to use a piece of cottonwood. It was not the best choice because it was as soft as the fire board and would heat up as well. He chopped off a hand-sized piece and flattened one side. Then he drilled a start hole for the upper end of the drill spindle in the flat side.

Wind in the Grass twisted the fire spindle into the loose bow string. It flexed the bow just enough to keep the string taut. He put the hand-sized piece of wood on top of the drill spindle, held the lower tip on the start hole in the fire board, and began drilling back and forth. As the wood drilled into the boards, it heated up.

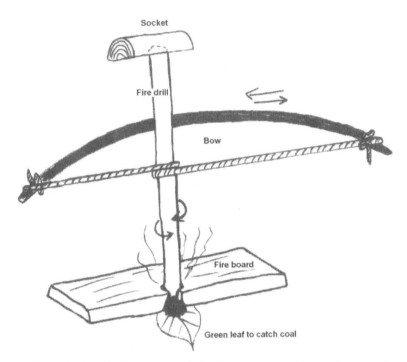

Once he had holes burned into the upper and lower boards, he stopped. He carved the upper end of the spindle down to a smaller point to reduce friction. Then he rubbed the tip of the spindle next to his nose and behind his ear so that his natural skin oils would slick that end up a bit. Then he carved a narrow "v" shaped notch in the fire board from the edge of the board to the center of the hole. This would be where the coal formed. He set a green leaf under the notch on the ground so he could pick up the coal after it had formed.

It was harder to work the bow drill from a sitting position instead of the usual kneeling position. He managed to get the hot sawdust to build up in the notch, which eventually began to smoke. He gently exhaled on the coal until it glowed red.

Wind then grabbed the nest of dried grass and rotted wood he had made earlier and gently slid the coal off the green leaf carrier into the center of the nest. As he breathed ever so gently on the coal, it began to heat up the rotten wood. This took a little while as he manipulated the nest to direct the heat into the center of rotted wood, dried grass, and leaves. The leaves began to smoke heavily as the coal worked its way down through them. Finally, the nest burst into flames. He set it inside the tipi of small twigs. Watching closely, he fed it with small sticks, progressing to larger ones as the fire grew. Before long, he had a warming fire.

Once the fire was burning, he draped his robe over one of the downed trees to dry it out. The reflection of heat off the boulder on one side and the logs with the robe over them on the other warmed his body. Wind in the Grass would make it through the night. Tomorrow he would find something to eat.

Morning came slower than usual. His night had been a rough one. As the shock of his injuries wore off, his pain was constant now. He could get water, but food was a problem. He could not move enough to gather vegetation up the hill. He had no way of catching a fish where the river was deep. He needed to stay close to the water because water would keep him alive even without food. Yet without food, he would grow weak. Also on his mind was the threat of the bear, which he figured was not far away. He had to move again.

Wind gathered more sticks and tightly lashed his leg. He cut off part of his long shirt for more lacing. He had to keep the leg from bending and dislocating his broken bones while moving. He could pack everything he would need each night, even if he only made a short distance during the day.

Moving uphill from the creek seemed daunting. He moved south along the creek until he reached an impassable boulder field blocking his way. Exhausted, he sat down and started a new fire with the bow drill kit he had made the day before. He had managed to gather some edible leaves on his way, but no other food was available. He drank long and hard before settling in for another night. Thankfully, his robe had dried out and was comforting to him. He sat against a boulder and fell asleep.

The next morning he assessed his situation. Nobody knew where he was and no one would miss him until they were packed to head south for the winter. Even then, they would not look for a scout of his skill. He was not going to heal quickly enough to return to his people before they left. He was injured in enemy territory, the bear was not far away, and it obviously had a liking for fighting humans.

He pondered the mystery of his fate. He had come to this place to see if he could understand the boy who hunted with wolves. He wondered if the boy could speak. If he could, what language might he use? Would it be a language Wind in the Grass would recognize or would it be the language of a people Wind had not encountered yet? Was he actually of the people who had been attacked last spring or had he and the wolves moved to the area after that attack had happened? He had too many questions to answer.

Now he figured that the small boy may be his only hope. He knew how dangerous wolves could be. Would the wolves that hunted with the boy accept him too? Would they try to protect the boy from him? He had no choice but to ask for the boy's help while he still had strength. He hoped the boy had connections to others who might help, although it seemed unlikely.

Wind in the Grass couldn't think about that now. He had to concentrate on what he could immediately accomplish. Slowly standing up, he hobbled up the hill. His leg was in extreme pain, and the first little bank away from the river was quite steep. With his first attempt, he lost his grip and balance and rolled back down the embankment, hitting his head on a rock. He lay there for a while, then tried to move but was now dizzy, weak, and in pain. He crawled back to his fire pit, added some limbs and leaned back against the rock he had sat at all night. He let the heat from the fire warm him and figured he would be there another night.

Just then, he became aware of at least two wolves staring at him from up the bank under the brush. He froze, not moving his head or even his eyes, but rather watching with his peripheral vision. He thought now that the whole pack would be there and he would have a fight on his hands. The second wolf turned to leave and his head came into view. It had a tattered ear!

Wind recognized it as one of the wolves the boy hunted with. The first wolf moved back and vanished. It never revealed if it was walking on three legs. The two creatures simply melted back into the forest and vanished. He felt hopeful. Perhaps there was not a larger pack after all. He would drink his fill in the morning and try again.

The next morning he felt less depressed, although the pain in his leg was just as acute. He had concluded he had to work his way cross country or die trying. It was better than dying while sitting there doing nothing. This time, he crawled up the steep slope dragging his belongings wrapped in his blanket. He made about a hundred yards through rough terrain before it leveled. He worked from sun up to sundown, but made little progress toward his goal of the plateau above the canyon where the marmot colony was. He figured if he could make it, the boy would find him there. At his current rate of travel, it would take many days to reach the marmot colony. He could find some edible leaves now and roots that could be easily dug up, but water would be less available. He kept moving until nearly dark, then stopped and built a small fire. He was still within sight of the previous night's camp.

Wind in the Grass made a mental game of setting a goal and trying to reach it in a day. The next couple of days, he made some progress. He licked moisture from the leaves and grasses in the mornings and once he even found a small rivulet of water seeping from a spring. He drank all he could hold.

Each night he built a fire for warmth and comfort. He worried about the enemy seeing the fire's light at night, but the fire was a deterrent to the bear, too, and he was more afraid of the bear at this point.

Wind in the Grass tried to measure his progress. He was getting closer to the plateau where the marmot colony lived. After three days' travel, he figured he was over halfway there. He thought about how an injury can turn a simple day's walk into a week-long journey.

His training in survival was being put to the test now. He had adjusted his leg wrappings and although his pain was constant, he was now able to manage it. He concentrated on the movements he had to do to gain a foot or so of travel. He was deep in concentration when he suddenly felt he was being watched. A little over a decent bow shot away, under a tree, the wolf with the tattered ear rested, watching Wind as he crawled in great pain. Wind thought he was laughing and enjoying the show. When the wolf noticed he had been seen, he got up and left. Wind then resumed his movement patterns. The wolf began showing up daily, seemingly to check on Wind's progress. For Wind it became something to look forward to each day.

Laughing Wolf, for his part, was just curious. He came without Mother because she would have led him away from the man. Laughing Wolf wondered why Mother thought this human posed a threat. He could barely move. The young wolf got braver each day and was soon sitting a short distance to the side of the man. The man started talking to the young wolf, trying to coax him closer. Laughing Wolf was not afraid, but he knew better than to get too close.

CHAPTER FIFTEEN

Company

One day when Mother had been gone for a while, Boy noticed Laughing Wolf was leaving and heading north. He grabbed his bag and spear and followed.

Laughing Wolf knew Boy was following, but did not wait. Boy had to jog to keep the pup within sight even though Laughing Wolf was not moving much faster than a deliberate trot. Laughing Wolf seemed to know where he was going and with a purpose.

Boy followed, but stopped short when he saw what Laughing Wolf was up to. He was now sitting on a hill looking down the slope watching a man!

The man had not spotted the boy, so Boy took cover behind a bush. The man spoke to the pup as if he knew him, but Laughing Wolf did not go to him. Still, he seemed to know this man's limitations and did not take cover.

The man slowly crawled up the hill, dragging one leg behind him, wrapped tightly with sticks and straps. Burdened with his injured leg and a heavy robe he carried in a bundle, he was making very little progress.

Boy did not recognize the words the man spoke to Laughing Wolf. Could this be an enemy? He was certainly not dressed like any people Boy had ever seen. The man's shirt was made with a different cut than the men he had known.

Boy watched the man for the rest of the day, even though at some point Laughing Wolf had left to continue his exploration. The man moved short distances, and then spent a long time resting. He was obviously weak. Boy figured he would not live much longer. He was still watching as the sun began setting. Boy was thinking about sneaking away when the man started unpacking his robe. Boy wanted to know what the man was carrying. The man quickly gathered some small tinder, made a ball of it and then pulled out his bow drill set, and drilled up a coal which he blew into flame in the tinder ball. Boy was fascinated but the light was leaving quickly, and he had his own fire to attend to.

Boy hurried back to his cave in the dark. Mother joined him about half way back and kept by his side. She lay down in the mouth of the cave while Boy tended his fire. Many thoughts ran through his mind. Would the man's people search for him? Were they the enemies? Or was he running from the enemy? Should Boy help the man? From watching the man, Boy had learned how to start a fire. If he let the man die, he could claim his robe and other belongings, but without the knowledge the man possessed, Boy may not be able to learn the secrets of fire making.

If the man was an enemy, Boy could be killed. But the man needed help. If the man survived, and asked to live with Boy and the wolves, would the wolves accept him? Would they have enough food for an extra person to last the winter?

After a fitful sleep, Boy decided that knowledge was much more valuable than whatever tools the man had wrapped up in his robe. Boy decided to try to help the man. If the man was not friendly, he could simply walk away and let fate take its course.

He packed his spear, his carry bag, and some dried meat and left at daybreak. Laughing Wolf and Mother came with him, the pup at his side and Mother out in front, but keeping track of them. Once Mother figured out where the boy was going, she tried to distract him and lead him away. Boy stopped and looked into her eyes. He thought how she must be concerned for his safety. He appreciated her concern, but he had made up his mind. When he turned back toward where the man had been the night before, Mother understood and did not object again. She hung back and watched. She would protect both her cubs should the man attack.

Boy found Wind in the Grass had moved only a short distance from where he had been the night before. He was trying to crawl, and although he was making progress, he was weak and dehydrated from crawling for so many days.

Boy approached quietly and stood a little back with his spear in hand. The man was older than he had looked from a distance. He was not very aware of his surroundings. Laughing Wolf moved in and circled the man. Wind noticed the wolf had come in closer than usual. Hesitating, he turned to make sure the wolf meant no harm. As he turned to sit up, he was startled to look into the eyes of the small boy. The boy held his spear up in a threatening manner, showing the old man he could kill him then and there if need be. The man looked down and held out his hands, palm up, in a submissive manner. Boy understood the gesture. He lowered his spear and reached into his bag, grabbed some dried meat and tossed it into the hands of the old man. The man did not look up, but ate half the meat, then put the other half in his rolled up robe as if he intended to save it for later.

The boy grunted and the man looked up at him again. The old man had tears in his eyes. He cupped his hands and made a motion as if he were drinking. Boy understood the man was thirsty and turned to point toward the nearest stream. The man made the gesture again. Boy thought about it a while. The man wanted him to bring water. He was not sure how he would do that. He had given water to Mother in a stone with a natural indentation. That was all he could figure to do, but it didn't hold much water. He ran to the river to see what he could find.

Mother watched from a distance as the boy and man met. She did not trust the man. She knew he was hurt and did not pose a threat to her or her pups, if they didn't get too close, but the boy was getting close. She was relieved when the boy headed for the creek. She waited and watched the man. Laughing Wolf followed Boy.

Boy found a small rock with an indentation and carefully filled it with water. He slowly returned to the old man and set down the rock just out of the man's reach, then backed off. Wind crawled to it and sipped the water. There was barely enough to wet his throat. He sat up and backed off again. The boy went for another trip. Wind now knew the boy had no container for water.

When Boy left for another water run, Wind looked around and saw a small, dead tree limb about as big around as his arm. He crawled to it and took out his war axe. He chopped out a section about twice as long as his hand, and then flattened one side. He then set up camp and was getting out his bow drill when the boy returned.

Seeing the old man had moved, the boy brought him the little bit of water he had carried. This time he walked right up to the old man and handed him the rock. The man drank the water again, then proceeded to start a fire. The boy watched closely and examined every step. Once the man had the fire going, he gestured to the boy to sit across from him at the fire. Boy did. Laughing Wolf approached and sat down next to boy. This did not really surprise the old man, but pleased him, by the look on his face. The humans stared at each other for a while. Boy noticed the well-made leather shirt the man wore. It had fringe along each arm and across the back. The bottom had hung nearly to his knees once but had been cut off unevenly. He had similar leather leg coverings, with fringe along the sides. They were held up by ties attached to his belt. His breechcloth was similar to Boy's, except larger. The flaps hung lower. The flaps were deco-rated with faded painting of designs Boy was not familiar with.

The old man's black hair was flecked with gray, showing his age. He had wrinkles in his face that reminded Boy of Two Bears. The boy wanted to trust the man, but he knew this old man could be an en-emy. The thought made him scoot back a bit further from the man.

Wind in the Grass noticed the boy was naked except for his old, tattered breechcloth. He probably had worn it for a long time. The boy was outgrowing it and it appeared to be too small. The boy's long flowing black hair was unkempt and ratty looking. The boy's eyes were inquisitive, yet had the look of knowing much more about life than a boy his age should.

Wind in the Grass again wondered if the boy spoke a language he might understand or if he spoke at all. He pointed to his own chest and stated his name. "Wind in the Grass." Then he pointed at the boy.

Boy was puzzled. He did not recognize the words the man had spoken and was not sure what he was trying to say. He chose to remain silent and continued looking at the man.

Wind added sticks to his fire and then pulled out the other half of the dried meat Boy had given him. He ate all of it this time. He picked up a stick about as big around as one of his fingers and about as long as his foot. Using his knife, he split the stick down the middle and thinned one end of each half. He placed a small twig between the thick ends and tied the two halves back together with short piece of cordage to make a set of tongs.

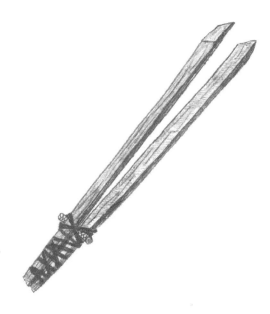

He then used them to pick up the biggest coal in the fire and set it on the flat side of the dead limb he had prepared. Slowly he began blowing on the coal as it began to burn the dead wood. Wind looked over at the boy, but the boy was looking at the war axe.

Boy had not noticed the axe until the man had used it to cut a green limb off a nearby tree. The axe was a sharp piece of rock that had been shaped, then set and tied into a wood handle. Boy had not remembered seeing such a tool. Neither Two Bears nor Talking Elk had owned one. Their axes were rough hand axes made of heavy stone. This was shaped well and considerably lighter, even with its wood handle. He was fascinated by it. Boy had pulled out more dried meat and was eating a piece himself as he admired the axe from a distance.

He finally noticed that the old man had used the green stick to grip the hot coal. The coal had burnt down into the piece of dead wood. The old man was manipulating the wood so he could blow on the coal and burn only in the direction he wanted it to. Once the original coal was burnt out, the old man added another coal and kept blowing. In what seemed like a very short time, the man had hollowed out the piece of wood to hold much more water than the rock had. Wind used a small sharp piece of stone to scrape clean much of the blackened area of the new burned-out bowl.

Holding the new bowl, Wind in the Grass indicated he was drinking from it. He handed it to the boy, who examined it closely. Here was a rough outer chunk of wood and the elongated inner bowl with the sides scraped smooth. The man had made it in less time than it took Boy to walk to the cave.

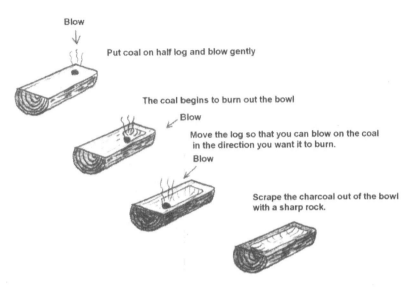

Blow

Put coal on half log and blow gently

The coal begins to burn out the bowl

Blow

Move the log so that you can blow on the coal in the direction you want it to burn.

Blow

Scrape the charcoal out of the bowl with a sharp rock.

Boy suddenly realized the man needed more water and had just made a tool for retrieving more water. Boy carried the bowl to the creek. The bowl indeed held much more water than the rock, and was easier to carry. He returned with the water for the old man.

The man drank it all and asked for more. Boy made another quick trip, and the man indicated his thirst was satisfied. He set the bowl down next to where he sat.

Wind was still trying to figure out if the boy could speak. If he did, he didn't seem to speak the language of Wind's people. He attempted to communicate again. He held up the bowl he had just made and said, "Bowl," then picked up the war axe and said, "axe." Then he again picked up the bowl and said, "bowl."

The boy said, "bowl" and the old man grinned. So the boy could speak!

The man tried his name again, pointing to the bowl, he said, "bowl" then pointing to himself, he said, "Wind in the Grass."

Boy understood that the man was trying to introduce himself. He said "Wind in the Grass" back to the old man just as he had said it. He didn't understand what the words meant but he could repeat them. The old man grinned and pointed to boy. He was asking for a name! Boy looked down. How could he give the man his name, when he had never been given a proper name? He thought for a moment and then pointed to himself and said "Boy" in the only language he had known, that of his captors, that of the enemy. Boy would have to be his official name until such time someone could name him properly.

The old man looked thoughtful, then said "Boy" in the boy's language. Wind then said "water thanks" in the boy's language. The boy grinned. The old man could speak his language! At least a little!

Wind in the Grass had watched the enemy people who spoke the language the boy was using. He had snuck up to the perimeter of their camp, watched and listened, trying to determine if the people were a threat to his clan. As a scout he had an acute interest in languages. He studied the languages of enemy and friendly people at every chance. He listened to their words and tried to mimic them in tone and inflection. He picked out words that he could tie to items and repeated them until he knew them. Over the years, he had picked up enough of the vocabulary of other tribes to be efficient at assessing whether they were a threat. He knew very few words of the boy's language, but he was confident that if the boy would stick around, he could communicate enough that they would understand each other. The language the boy spoke confused his theory as to why the boy was there and alone. Was he a captive of the people who had died there last spring? If so, why didn't he return to his own group? If not, why did he speak the language of an enemy people, when Wind knew the dead cave dwellers had spoken a different language? Perhaps the three warriors who had chased Wind into the bear were a search party sent out to find the boy. For what purpose? All these questions made Wind's head hurt.

Just then, the boy stood up and without a word, walked off in the direction he had come from. The pup fell in behind him. As they crested the hill, Mother joined them, and they were gone.

Wind in the Grass wondered if he had offended the boy. What had he done? He looked around. He had a half a day of daylight left, so he prepared his things and began to crawl again. This time, he packed the bowl in his bedroll so he would have it again if the boy returned.

He struggled the rest of the day, up until nearly nightfall before stopping to build another fire and try to get some sleep.

Boy had made a decision. He was going to try to help this man. He got up and headed to the cave. He would retrieve his blanket and more dried meat. He would try to get the man to follow him to his cave. It would be slow going along the steep ridge to get to the cave, but the man would have a better chance at survival if he made it to · the cave.

Fresh water, shelter, and food were available there and the boy would have fresh meat if the wolves hunted again or his traps worked. He knew he could learn a lot from this man, things he needed to know.

He returned to the cave and checked to make sure the fire would not completely go out if he was gone for an extended time. He packed some more meat and a handful of dried berries. Mother and Laughing Wolf followed him inside and watched as he prepared. Mother knew what he was going to do, and she was wary of the situation. She headed out to hunt on her own. Laughing Wolf followed her out, but then came back shortly. He would follow the boy and protect him if need be. They headed back toward the man.

The water and food had brought Wind back to a state of awareness. He could tell by the reaction of the small birds and critters around him that the wolf approached. Listening, he could tell the boy was walking not far behind. He said, "Greetings" in the boy's language before he saw them but when he knew they were within hearing distance. The boy appeared in the firelight and was astonished.

"How did you know I was there?" he asked, but the man did not answer. He asked the old man, "Do you talk like I do?"

The man replied, "Little."

The boy nodded.

Realizing that the old man was not one of the tribe that pursued him put Boy's mind at ease. He sat down next to Wind's fire and wrapped his wolf robe around himself. The old man smiled. Boy offered the man more meat and the man took it, stashing half with his gear and eating half right away.

Boy pointed to the fire and said, "Fire."

The man pointed to the fire and repeated the boy's word. Then he said "fire" in his own language.

The boy repeated the old man's word. They spent the night exchanging words and developing a sign language that allowed them to talk enough to get simple concepts back and forth.

Before he fell asleep, the boy managed to explain that he lived in a cave and invited the man to his home. He doubted the man understood how tough it might be getting there. The old man had accepted and indicated he would have to take his time because of his injured leg. The boy acknowledged the crippled man's concern and they lay down to sleep. Laughing Wolf curled up between Boy and the man. He did not fully trust this new human.

CHAPTER SIXTEEN

A New Teacher

In the morning, Boy tried to help the man stand, but Boy was too small to support his weight and the old man was too weak to support himself. He would have to crawl.

It took three more days of the man crawling carefully to reach the mouth of the cave. Boy left each day, returning to the cave to check the fire, and returning with dried meat to share. On the last day, he prepared a sleeping spot by the fire and a space for the old man's belongings. Boy also stored his own precious tools underneath his sleeping shelf so that the old man would recognize they were the boy's and not to be used without permission.

When Wind in the Grass finally crawled into the front of the cave, he was impressed with what the boy had accomplished. Firewood was stacked in preparation for winter. He noticed the drawings on the cave wall and realized it was a cave of the grandfathers. He looked toward the rear of the cave and saw through a low opening the three flat rocks. He had been in grandfather caves before, and correctly assumed the rocks to be the lids of storage bins. He figured this would be where the boy had the dried meat stashed that he had been bringing to him daily. He noticed the fish spear, crudely made yet quite functional. He looked with interest at the meat drying racks, the stacks of marmot hides and several dried deer hides. The boy was doing his best to prepare for winter, probably as he had seen his people do in the past.

Wind concluded the boy did not know how to tan a deer hide, but was smart enough to scrape and save the hides. And best of all, the small creek running along the cave floor meant drinking water was right at their feet! It was a perfect wintering cave. The wolves had obviously lived there with him for some time as their tracks were scattered throughout the cave.

The boy had cleared a spot on the floor for the old man. Exhausted, Wind lay down to sleep even though he had arrived midday. Boy let him sleep. Mother and Laughing Wolf were out again. Boy left to check his traps. He also wanted to look for just the right dead wood to try and make a bowl like Wind in the Grass had done.

Wind awoke and found himself alone. He felt grateful for his new friend. He was not sure yet whether the wolves were his friends. He vowed not to interfere with the boy's relationship with the wolves. It was a unique situation—the very thing he had come to study. It was what got him in the position of being dependent on this small tribe, or pack, or whatever it might be called.

Wind figured he had to earn his keep. He had earned his own way all his life and hard work never had daunted him. His damaged leg would keep him from participating in the activities he normally would have done. He had to keep his leg wrapped and allow it to heal. He wasn't sure if he would be able to walk correctly ever again. He hoped his leg would be healed by spring so he could meet up with his people. They would accept him back and provide for him based on his past service.

He knew they would need a larger bowl or cooking pot and a tool or two for working the hides. Before winter set in, the boy would need a long shirt and leggings at least. Wind could make these things, but he would need the boy to gather materials. He would probably have to teach the boy just what to look for. He began preparing a mental list.

His first priority would be to allow his leg to heal. But also as important was learning to communicate with the boy. He would need sleep for a while to allow his body to heal itself. He lay down and fell into a deep sleep.

When Boy returned from checking his traps, he grabbed his fish spear and went down to the river. He did not find any fish large enough to spear. He wondered why. Last fall, he remembered the men catching large fish and the woman drying them. Had they caught all the larger fish in the river? Frustrated, he walked downriver further than he had in the past.

He came to a spot where a large patch of the green plant that stung blocked his way. The leaves were serrated, and the plant was covered with fuzzy hairs. It was the plant that Fire Woman had used to make string. He would remember this patch for later.

Avoiding the patch of stinging plants, he started walking uphill away from the river. He was about half way up when he discovered a black, shiny rock with a sharp edge sticking out of the ground. He looked further and found other black rock that was neither sharp nor shiny. He picked up one of these nodules about the size of Mother Wolf's head and smashed it against one about the same size still on the ground. It shattered into many pieces. They were all shiny on the inside and all of the edges were extremely sharp.

Boy knew he had found the same kind of rock that had been used to make his knife. He looked up and down the ridge, but there was only a small vein of cobble rising out of the hill. He picked up another nodule small enough that he could carry, and headed back to the cave. He wasn't sure how, but he figured he could make another knife from the rock if he tried.

Mother and Laughing Wolf had stumbled on a real challenge. Traveling west of the cave, they had crossed a canyon and headed to higher elevation. They smelled blood and went to investigate. They found an old bull elk with huge antlers. Bloodied along his left side, he was weak and lying down next to a small stream. Mother figured he had used the last of his strength in a fight with a younger bull that probably had head gear just as big as his. The other elk had left with the prize of a female ready to breed. The old bull was waiting to die and would not survive the winter. The other bull had punctured his lung with a forceful jab through the side of the old bull's rib cage. The fight had depleted the oxygen in his blood and he had lost the use of his hind legs. When the old bull collapsed, the younger bull had twisted his head a few more times with his antlers to make sure the old bull understood who had won. The younger bull left with his prize, but would probably have to fight again to defend her.

Mother figured she would speed up this elk's death. First, she came in from behind the bull to see if he would get up. He didn't. He swung his antlers toward her but was so weak that he was slow. Laughing Wolf ran in and bit him on the flank. The bull attempted to get up, but couldn't. Mother circled to the front of the bull and waited for her opportunity. Laughing Wolf, getting a feel for this hunt, went for the bull's throat, but was rewarded with a sharp jab from a tilted antler. The bull still had some fight left in him. Laughing Wolf moved behind the bull and tried to bite the back of his neck. The bull responded by leaning his antlers back. That was what Mother needed. She rushed in and grabbed him by the throat. He struggled to get loose, but she had him in a death grip, choking down his breathing. Laughing Wolf now had his full weight on the bull's shoulders and was biting the back of its neck. Laughing Wolf wasn't helping much, but the extra weight was enough to limit the bull's struggling. In a short period of time it was over. Mother ripped open his belly and they ate their fill.

They headed back to the cave with blood on their fur. Mother thought that a full pack would have eaten the bull in one evening. Tomorrow she would lead the boy back to the kill. He would want the hide. He would also bring meat back to the cave as he had before. They would get another few days' of eating if a bear or the birds didn't find it too soon.

Boy had returned to the cave. He set down his fish spear along with the rock. He pulled out some dried meat for the evening and shared it with Wind in the Grass when he awoke. The fire was built up and they were teaching each other their words for different things in the cave when Mother and Laughing Wolf returned. Right away Boy and Wind noticed the smell of fresh blood, and Boy knew they had made a kill of a large animal. Mother came close to Boy and looked him in the eyes. He looked back. That was all they needed to communicate that he had work to do in the morning. Laughing Wolf plopped down between Wind and the boy and began giving himself a bath, licking his fur clean of the sticky blood. Mother moved to the back of the cave away from the fire and started cleaning herself as well.

Boy let Wind know that he would be going after what meat he could carry in the morning. Wind asked if he could cut off a leg at the knee joint and bring one back. Boy was puzzled. The meat was not thick there and it was tough. The upper leg would have better meat, and more than he could carry in one trip. Wind indicated he wanted the bone to make a tool, so the boy said he would bring one.

At daybreak Mother led Boy out of the cave and they made good time reaching the kill in about an hour. Boy was amazed! It was a huge animal. He wondered how Mother ever brought down this one.

He could not know of the fight that occurred before she had arrived on the scene. He remembered the old man's request and took a leg first, then skinned out the upper side of the animal. He realized there was no way he was going to carry the hide and meat in one trip. Cutting strips of meat from near the backbone, he filled his carry bag. He cut large chunks of meat from the upper hip and started back to the cave. It took him until midmorning to get back. Boy told Wind as much as he could about the kill. Wind asked how big the antlers were. Boy said it would be all he could do to carry back the head and antlers. He wouldn't even be able to carry the whole hide back he figured. Wind told him to take a sharp hammer stone, crack the skull, and use the antlers as leverage to try to break off one to bring back if he could. He told him the brain could be used to make the hide soft, but that would be harder to pack and impossible to store. Boy left the meat in the cave with Wind and went back after more.

Wind began cutting and drying the meat on the drying rack. He took the meat that Boy had cut from along the backbone and carefully separated the wide, flat sinew from both pieces. He set this aside to dry flat, and then cut the meat into thin strips. He also cooked a large chunk for the evening meal. Then he skinned out the lower legs with the knife he carried as his main survival tool. A tendon ran up the back of the leg in a groove in the bone. This he cut out, keeping as much of the length as he could and set it out to dry. The thick, round white cords would be hammered and separated into sinew fibers to use for sewing thread and to make strong cordage. He cut off the hooves and set them aside to dry. These could be used as decorations or rattles for making music.

The bones were cleaned. He found an edge of a stone where he could begin grinding the edge of one of the bones and started working it. This would make a good hide scraper, but it had to be sharpened. He broke off one end by crushing it with the hammer stone, and then ground it down on the rough grinding stone. When the end was angled off to one bone edge, he used his stone knife to serrate the end. This would be a hand scraper.

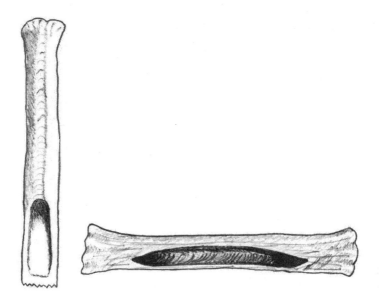

On another leg bone he worked on the flatter side of the bone where the tendon had grown in the groove. It took work to get the smooth bone to start wearing away, but once it did, the job went faster. On the abrading stone he wore into the soft middle of the bone. He ate the marrow from inside, a fatty treat. The effect was a tool that could be used on a hide against a log for greater scraping effect.

Later in the day, the boy arrived with another load of meat. He said he had tried to get the antler loose, but he was not strong enough. Wind understood. The boy ate some of the meat that Wind had cooked, then headed back. This time he was after what he could carry of the hide. It took him the rest of the day, but he was back by dark. He had a little over half of the elk hide. He tossed it down as he came in the cave. He was tired and bloody. He went outside and down the hill to a deeper part of the stream and washed himself. He returned to warm himself by the fire and to eat more cooked elk meat.

Wind had sharpened the bone enough to work on the hide. He asked the boy to drag one of the larger logs that had been brought in for firewood over to him. He positioned it from the ground up onto his lap and then laid the hide hair-side down over the log. He began scraping the last of the meat and fat off the underside of the hide. It took him until well after dark, but with the new scrapers, he removed the flesh down to just the white hide. Boy watched with interest and saw how much faster the tools made the process than he had been able to do it with a stone scraper on the deer hides.

All of the companions were tired. Laughing Wolf was already curled up. Mother was outside the mouth of the cave curled up and keeping watch. Boy lay down in his robe and watched as Wind folded the elk hide together, hair out, and then rolled it up. He then put the hide away from the fire to keep it as moist as he could. He would have put it in the creek below the cave if he had been able to walk. It would mean more work but he could get it done if he started early tomorrow. He lay down in his robe for the night too.

The next day, Boy headed out on another trip to the carcass for more meat. Wind began removing the hair from the elk hide. He put the hide over his lap with the hair facing up this time. He started working the hide from the area closest to the bull's neck and working back toward his rump, moving in the same direction that the hair grew. Fresh hides that had not dried out completely always scraped easier. Once they had dried, they would have to be soaked in a stream to rehydrate them in order to remove the hair. This hide was still soft enough, with only a few spots that had dried too much. Wind had stripped the hide by the time Boy returned with his first load of meat. Boy was impressed with the amount of work Wind was doing even without the use of one leg.

Boy returned for one more load. Wind started scraping the flesh side of the hide again, trying to remove as much membrane as he could. It scraped easier now that there was no cushion of hair between the hide and the log. He set the hide in the cave water downstream from the drinking hole. He cleaned up the hair mess he had made and piled it up so boy could haul it outside when he returned. Wind continued to strip and dry meat as the day went on.

Boy had company from the start with the wolves coming for another meal and to watch boy work the carcass. This time boy was after the head. He couldn't crack the skull so he used his knife to separate the vertebrae and remove the whole head from the body. He skinned it out as best he could to lighten the weight and began dragging the antler and skull back to the cave. It weighed about half of the boy's own weight. It took him longer to carry than the meat because the antler tines got caught in the brush and made moving more difficult. By the time Boy made it back to the cave with the head and antlers, he was exhausted. He cleaned up, lay down across from Wind, and watched him as he went about drying meat.

After a while Wind grabbed one of the antlers and dragged the skull over closer to him. Boy got up to offer his hand axe. Wind took the stone tool and chipped away at the skull until he had a deep groove most of its length. He then got boy to tug on the end of one antler while he pulled on the other. The skull cracked in two pieces, exposing the brain. Wind grabbed the scraped hide and unrolled it. He took the brain and smashed it into the hide as it lay stretched out on the floor. Although the smell of the brains was beginning to bother Boy, he watched with interest. Once the whole hide had been covered with crushed brains, Wind folded up the hide again.

He asked the boy to bring him two strong sticks and one of the old deer hides from the back of the cave. Boy went outside in search of sticks. He cut two about the length of his arm and as big around as his wrist. He brought them and the old hide to Wind. The old hide he soon found out was to catch the drippings. Wind unfolded the scraped hide, folded it in a loop around one of the sticks as Boy held it. He rolled the sides in towards the center of the hide tucking in any loose ends and stuck the other stick through the center. He had Boy hold one stick as he twisted the other until he squeezed the brains right through the hide and they dripped on the old hide. He kept turning and wringing until the hide was all squeezed out.

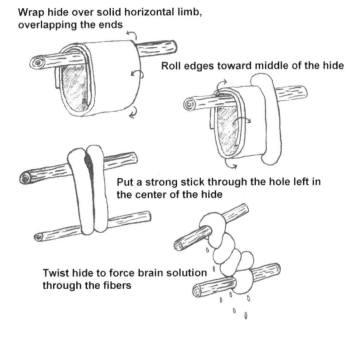

Wrap hide over solid horizontal limb, overlapping the ends

Roll edges toward middle of the hide

Put a strong stick through the hole left in the center of the hide

Twist hide to force brain solution through the fibers

Unwrapping the elk hide, Wind used it to soak up what he could of the brain juice from the old hide. He folded it onto the stick again and did the process all over. He repeated until the two hides had soaked in what brains were left. The last time, he rubbed what was left of the brain mixture on the old hide as evenly as he could. He told the boy to let brains dry there. It would help later.

Wind in the Grass then washed his hands and grabbed the fresh hide, pulling and stretching it in all directions. He worked the edges by stretching them with his fingers to loosen the fibers as the hide started to dry. He enlisted the boy's help to stretch the hide one way, then the other. They kept this up for a long time. Boy was getting tired of this part of hide tanning. Then all of a sudden, the hide fluffed up, was whiter and softer to the touch. It still felt a bit damp and cool to the touch. Wind said this was the critical part because if it was not completely dry it would not stay soft. Even though he felt fatigued, Boy kept up the stretching process with Wind until the hide dried. The hide no longer felt cold to the touch, and most of it fluffed up into a soft, white blanket. Some of the hide's thicker areas—like the rump and neck—felt soft to the finger, but were a bit stiff to the hand. Boy liked the feel of it and the white color was unusual. Wind folded the hide in half lengthwise, then borrowing the boy's awl and rawhide string, he stitched up the edges to form an open-ended bag. He set it aside for now.

He explained to Boy that if the hide got wet now, it would return to rawhide, so he would have to smoke the hide, which would keep it soft but change the color to a golden brown. For the smoking process, Wind needed a supply of rotten wood—the kind that crumbled when handled. Boy said he would find some tomorrow. Wind also need three long poles and some string to suspend the hide above a hole in the ground. Tomorrow Boy would hunt for three useable poles as well.

The morning was bright and sunny but a bit on the chilly side. It didn't take Boy long to find what Wind needed, but chopping the poles out of a pole patch with his hand axe took some time. After he had carried the poles back near the cave, he laid them out in three directions, crossing a couple feet of the top of each pole, as Wind had told him. Lashing the poles together where they crossed, he lifted the center of the tripod as high as he could to get it to stand by itself. He pushed each leg one at a time until the tripod stood at its full height. Boy dug a pit about twice as wide as his hand and three times as deep directly under the center of the poles.

Wind instructed Boy to bring a bed of coals from the cave fire, add wood, and let it burn down to coals. With Wind's instruction, Boy used his roll of twine Fire Woman had made and threw it over the tripod. Tying the end of the string to the closed end of the softened hide, he pulled it up in the air above the fire. When the coals were good and hot, he covered them with rotten cottonwood and then lowered the hide down over the hole. Wind explained that evergreen wood, even when rotten, tended to contain too much resin and would burn too hot. A too-hot fire could cook and shrivel the hide or at least turn it a black color. Using rotten wood from trees that lost

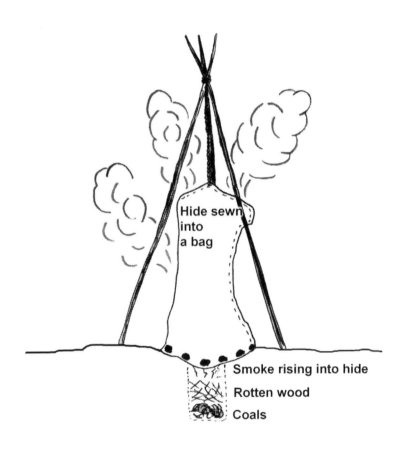

Hide sewn into a bag

Smoke rising into hide

Rotten wood

Coals

their leaves each fall would burn with less heat and give the hide a golden brown color.

Boy flared out the open end of the hide and covered the fire hole so all the smoke generated by the rotten wood was captured within the hide. Putting rocks on the edges of the hide where it touched the ground forced the smoke to go through the hide, not around it. The hide kept the fire from getting too much air so it smoldered, producing much more smoke, rather than bursting into flame. He let the hide absorb smoke until Wind thought he could pull it inside out and give the other side the same treatment.

Boy took down the hide, and turned it inside out. The smoked side of the hide had turned golden brown. Boy smoked the other side until Wind told him it should be finished. Boy brought the hide down and removed the stitching, saving cordage as he went. Wind trimmed any stiff edges from the hide, and then had Boy take the hide down to the creek and give it a thorough washing.

When Boy brought it back, Wind said, "Now let us soften what little stiffness is left in the hide."

They started the stretch-and-dry process all over. This time did not take as long and the hide turned quite soft. Wind explained that on a big hide like the elk, it may take two or three attempts to work the hide soft. Wind would never be able to stretch a hide that big by himself. Boy was a great help. Wind assured Boy that deer hides would be easier if they could soak them and get the hair off and then brain each hide while it was soft and wet. Wind rolled up the finished hide and set it next to his sleeping area. Boy took two of the older, dry hides down to the creek and anchored them under water with rocks. He would bring each one to Wind as he requested. Removing the hair was a job Wind could work on a little at a time while his leg was healing.

CHAPTER SEVENTEEN

Learning to communicate

Mother and Laughing Wolf spent more and more time out roaming. They stopped by and checked on the humans in the cave when they were near, but now that Wind in the Grass had moved in, Boy was spending much more time with him than the wolves. Mother thought they made a lot of odd sounds back and forth to each other as they busied themselves with tasks she did not comprehend.

Laughing Wolf was nearly full grown now and was an accomplished hunter. He would soon have to deal with other wolves. He returned howls to others far off at night as they sang. One day Mother and Laughing Wolf encountered a single male wolf that was on an exploratory trip into what Mother considered her territory. She recognized the male as a lesser male from her original pack. They approached each other and sniffed a greeting. Mother did not show submissiveness as she had held a higher position than this wolf when she knew him last. He accepted her attitude but did not show submissiveness either, as he considered her an equal at this point. His pack had an alpha male and female he would submit to.

Laughing Wolf bounded up to meet the new wolf but found he was greeted with a fight! The big wolf bit him harshly for his insolence and took him down in a scrapping tussle until the pup rolled onto his back and lay still. He instinctively showed his underbelly to show the big male he submitted to his dominance. Mother watched anxiously but did not interfere. It was a lesson the pup needed to learn. She knew she held the respect of the other wolf and he would

149

not seriously hurt the pup with her near. Once Laughing Wolf was let up, he stood back away from the two adults. They looked at each other for a short time before the big male ran back the way he had come. He stopped once to see if the female would follow, but when he saw she was not interested, he disappeared into the vegetation to return to the pack.

Laughing Wolf was not so eager to return howls after that incident. He and Mother continued to hunt and to put on fat for the winter, eating as much and as often as they could. It was their way of surviving the winter. It was the same for the animals they hunted. The bears were active too, but Mother avoided the bigger predator, especially one with scars on his nose and two missing claws. That one was just plain mean.

As Wind in the Grass healed, he and Boy shared their languages more. Boy was a quick study, and the two began to carry on conversations beyond the basics. Wind let Boy know he had watched as he and the wolves killed the fawn last spring. The joint effort was so out of the ordinary Wind was sure spirits must have been tricking his eyes. The sight so concerned him he had left his clan to study Boy and the wolves to try to make sense of what he had seen. Wind had not told his people about the sighting because he was not sure if it had been real or a vision. He had been relieved when he saw Boy was real and so were the wolves. He told Boy about leaving the deadfall trap so Boy could find it. He shared his story about encountering the three enemy warriors who had come dangerously near the boy's cave, and how he had led them away, but had been careless running into the old bear. Wind had been lucky when the bear pursued the warriors, giving him a chance to escape. He had been even luckier when Boy found him.

When the subject of Boy's name came up, Boy told Wind that he had never earned a name. Fire Woman and the men had just used "Boy" in the language they spoke. He told Wind he had hoped he would be able to spend more time with the men this year and be able to distinguish himself with a deed that would have earned him a name. He had dreamed that Two Bears would name him and tell stories of how he had come by a good name to replace Boy. Wind in the

Grass knew that the boy's dream would not come true because Two Bears was gone.

Boy told Wind the story of how he had been left in the cave, the sounds of the battle, how Mother Wolf had appeared when he emerged from his hiding place. She had been near death and he had nursed her back to health because of the loneliness he felt. He told Wind of the other pup and how it had died, how he had felt the danger from outside the cave and returned to find the large cat in the cave. He explained what he had done and how that experience had made Mother and pup trust him completely. He told about finding the big cat's body later. He brought out the two cat claws to prove his story. Wind showed his two bear claws, and they laughed.

Wind reminded Boy of Two Bears. Both older men knew much more than they showed. Boy was learning much from Wind.

Wind had come to unravel a mystery. He had heard Boy's story and was satisfied with the explanation. He told Boy he would spend the winter in the cave because it would take that long before he could walk well enough to travel back to his own people. His people would not return to the area until next spring. He told Boy about how he learned Talking Elk's fate and how he had pursued the enemy to his last breath. He also told the boy he did not find any sign of Fire Woman. He suggested she probably was still with her captors working as a slave again.

It was then that Boy began remembering his unhappy childhood. He could remember being separated from the other children. He and Fire Woman had to work for the others, the people she called the "Bear Eaters." Fire Woman spoke a different language than the Bear Eaters. She had spoken some of those words to Boy when he was small, but he didn't remember many now. She referred to her own clan as the "True People." Boy had only spoken the language of the Bear Eaters as long as he could remember, although they treated him as a captive rather than one of their own. Fire Woman had taken care of Boy for as long as he could remember. They had run away together to try to find the True People, but instead they found Talking Elk and Two Bears. These two men belonged to a tribe Fire Woman called the "Fish Eaters." The men spoke the language of the Fish Eaters but also of the True People. They knew enough of the Bear Eaters' language to speak with Boy.

They had been attacked in the night and forced to run again. That is how they had ended up in this cave during a snowstorm last winter. Because they had lost all their possessions, they had begun making new tools and weapons with what they could find above the snow. Boy thought they lived a decent life for a time. The men, who were good hunters, had made hunting spears and had been proficient at using them.

In the spring they had planned to travel again, but the enemy attacked before they were ready to leave. Fire Woman hid the boy while the men fought outside the cave. That was the last he had seen of any of them.

Wind listened without speaking. He knew the boy was bringing up this story from a place in his memory he hadn't visited in a very long time and it was a painful place to be. He nodded and thought about the story.

He said, "You have a mystery past, and like all of us, your future is a mystery. But you also are living in the mystery of your life now, knowing a friendship with wild wolves. I do not know where life will take you, but it is clear you have a special journey to travel. What I believe is, I saw you last spring and therefore was brought here for a reason beyond my own control. Our lives were meant to cross paths in this time and this place. I will give to you all that I can to help you in the next step of your journey. It will be between you and your guiding spirits as to what your next step will be. Mine will be to return to my people next spring, providing I make it through this coming winter."

Boy looked into Wind's eyes and saw the sincerity in his words. He said quietly, "I know."

The next day Wind crawled to the front of the cave and listened intently. He watched the birds flying. He turned to boy and asked, "Is your fish spear a good one?"

Boy replied, "It is good enough."

"Good!" said wind. "I suggest you take it and your gathering bag down to the river this morning!"

Boy looked at him, puzzled.

Wind said, "They won't wait for you."

Gathering his spear, bag, and knife, Boy headed down the stream to where it intersected the main river. He couldn't believe his eyes. The river was full of really big fish! He started fishing and immediately skewered a fish so big it took all his strength to work it to the shore and drag it onto the bank. Picking up a large rock, he clubbed it on the head to stop it from flopping. In a short time, he caught four fish that were so big he would have to make two trips to carry them to the cave. Wind was ready with the drying racks. He showed Boy how to fillet the fish for drying. He cut down the center of the fish's back then along the ribs so the whole side peeled off in one slab. The slabs were cut smaller and hung on a rack to dry.

"How did you know?" boy asked Wind.

"The birds and the fish told me, "Wind replied.

"But how did they tell you?"

"In the way the birds reacted to the fish in the river and the sound of the fish swimming up the stream," Wind answered. "Now go get some more!"

Boy was amazed at Wind's ability to hear that far away and his understanding of the ways of the wild animals. He headed back. This time, he cut the fish into fillets on the riverbank and could haul more fish in his carry bag. He worked all day. Through the night they dried a good supply of fish.

Wind stayed up to keep the fire going. After several days of fishing, they had all the dried fish they could store. Boy had to dig a new storage pit to hold it all. Wind asked him to return all the fish bones to the river.

"This is how I thank the fish for the use of their flesh," Wind said, "and let them know I will appreciate them again next year if they choose to come back to this river."

Boy liked this concept. He made sure he returned every bit of unused fish to the water.

CHAPTER EIGHTEEN

Winter

Months passed. Wind limped around with the help of a strong branched-stick he used to support his weight. He had scraped the other deer hides, rolled them up, and set them aside, waiting for fortune to bring some deer brains to tan them. After the first snowfall, the wolves had made another kill on a large, old doe. Wind had Boy gather the tendons from all four legs, along with the hide and head. Wind soaked one of the older rawhides and tanned both it and the fresh hide with the doe's brains.

Using sinew thread pounded out of the leg tendons, Wind sewed a new shirt for Boy with the larger hide and part of the second. He also made Boy a larger breechcloth. The shirt had short fringe along the arms and along its base that would allow water to run off quicker and keep the winter wind from lifting an edge and blowing under the shirt. The boy had been nearly naked and with winter upon them, he needed clothing. Because Wind's leg was still healing, he figured he would spend the winter inside the cave. His blanket and the fire would keep him warm.

He used the large elk hide to make leggings for the boy. He made two pair of moccasins, one for the boy and a new set for himself. Knowing that Boy would have to go out in bad weather eventually, Wind in the Grass used some of the marmot hides to make a stiff winter hat and stiff outer mitten shells. The soft inner mittens he made from elk hide. These would keep the boy's hands warm enough to work when the time came.

155

Blowing snow piled up in front of the cave. Wind and the boy rolled wet snow into large balls they stacked to build a wall across the cave's entrance. They built it as tall as they could to break the cold wind from entering their living area. The blowing snow drifted over the wall, arching taller and taller, effectively sealing the cave from the weather. Through the snow wall Wind punched a small smoke hole open at the top northern edge. They kept a doorway dug open at the southern edge, closing it with a stiff hide during particularly bad storms. The draft of air flowing between these two openings, cold coming in the lower doorway and warmer air leaving through the smoke hole, kept the cave from filling with smoke.

With the first snowfall the wolves had returned to the cave and had stayed close by as winter moved in. Mother became more comfortable with the fire and trusted Boy to keeping it under control. She still didn't trust the old, crippled human who had moved into the cave, but the boy definitely had grown to trust him so she could live with that. Still, she did not let the old man touch her like she let the boy. As for Laughing Wolf, he slept next to Wind as often as he slept next to Boy. The wolves spent storms in the cave, but when the weather improved, went out on excursions. Boy shared equally with all of his pack the meat he had dried. Wind thought maybe the wolves should fend for themselves, but Boy was in charge. This was his cave and his work that had saved the dried meat in the first place.

Wind in the Grass' own clan kept dogs. They were probably part wolf, but they had been kept as livestock so long that the wild was mostly bred out of them. Mostly they were used to drag travois, two drag poles tied to a harness and attached to the dog. Sticks crossed the main drag poles behind the dog, forming a platform on which the people tied their belongings. When the people moved camp, the dogs dragged their owner's belongings. In lean times, the dogs could also be used for food. Dogs never were fed good meat like Boy was feeding these wolves. This prejudice was one that had been lifelong in Wind's mind. He was working hard to see the wolves as equals, but it just didn't sit right with him. Boy saw his struggle and explained that the wolves had hunted and killed as much of the meat as he had, if not more. They were keeping the humans alive as much as the humans were keeping them alive through preserving the earlier kills. Wind understood his logic, but a long-held prejudice was a hard thing to overcome.

On sunny days, the snow outside warmed up, then froze at night to form a hard crust. The wolves ran freely on top of the crusted snow. Sometimes the crust was even hard enough to allow Boy to walk on top. His moccasins kept his feet warm for a short time, but Wind showed him how to make them warmer with a little effort in gathering. He had Boy gather last summer's dead grass, dry it out by the fire, and stuff his moccasins with it. This insulated his skin from the cold snow even more. Wind in the Grass asked Boy to bring back evergreen boughs. With them he wove Boy a set of snowshoes that spread his weight out over the snow, making it easier for him to walk on top of the snow. It was a crude system and had to be rebuilt frequently, but it worked when he needed them. Sometimes he ventured out to get firewood, once or twice to follow Mother or Laughing Wolf on an excursion, but mostly he walked just to get out of the cave for a while.

Wind in the Grass was having a harder time keeping his attitude positive. He was walking better but could not negotiate the slick, snow-covered hillsides. He could get outside the door and sit in the sun to look at the winter view, but most of his time was spent in the cave. He told Boy many stories about his life and about his tribe. He told him his philosophy on his life as a scout and about different ways of understanding what was happening around him while he remained concealed from the view of other humans. He could not teach Boy the skills of concealment in the cave. Boy would have to practice outdoors. There were skills for winter concealment but more for summer concealment when the world was greener. He had never been so involved with another adult man and was learning much. Even with the confinement winter brought, he was having a good time.

One thing Wind taught Boy was flint knapping. Wind taught this skill on sunny days when both of them could get outside the cave for a while. They chose a spot that was easy for Wind to reach, and set up a log bench. The knapping bench was out of the way of normal traffic. The fine, sharp flakes would not be good inside the cave or where the wolves would walk across them. The stone Boy had brought back was a nodule of obsidian. It was good material for making knives and arrowheads.

Before he could teach the boy to flint knap, first Wind had to create a few tools. Wind used the hand axe to scar deer antlers at the

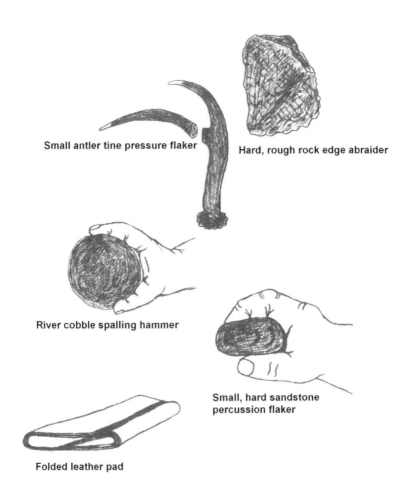

Small antler tine pressure flaker

Hard, rough rock edge abraider

River cobble spalling hammer

Small, hard sandstone percussion flaker

Folded leather pad

base of the tine. Once he had cut into them enough, he broke off the long, pointed tine and ground the base so it felt smooth in his hand. Wind sent Boy to the river to find hammer stones. They had to be rough to the touch but fine grained. He wanted several different sizes: larger stones for big flakes, smaller stones for small flakes. This sandstone was not soft, yet it absorbed some of the strike shock to the obsidian blade. The roughness caught the edge of the blade he was working to peel off flakes more consistently.

To protect his hand, he cut a couple of small pieces of the tanned deer hide. All this tool production took days, but he had the time and Boy was quite interested in helping and learning how it was done.

When he had his tools ready, Wind utilized the largest of the rounded river rocks as a hammer stone to initially break the obsidian nodule. He struck the large piece of glassy black rock just right to re-lease a large flake. This flake was thick at the end where it had been struck and thin at the opposite edge. It had a slight curved shape to it. Wind explained the knife blade was in this flake but that more flakes would have to be removed to thin the thick edge and shape a straight blade out of the curve.

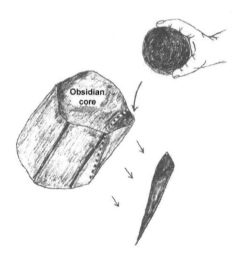

Wind struck the big rock again to get another flake. He called this process "spalling." He spalled several more large flakes off the main rock. On each large flake he ground the sharp edges dull with a rough rock. This was so he could handle the flake and not accidentally cut himself. He used a piece of soft leather to handle the rock as he worked with it.

After he had a few spalled flakes to work with, he picked up one of the larger flakes and used a smaller sandstone cobble to strike the edge to remove smaller flakes. He would work his way around the flake, picking the thicker ridges from previous flakes to remove another flake. Between strikes, he ground the sides of his emerging blade to dull them up and prepare them for the next strike.

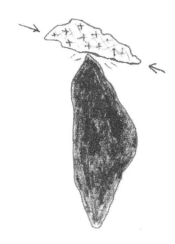

The grinding produced many little, sharp flakes but as Wind explained, the edge they were working on now could be strengthened by grinding shallow flakes off the underside first. Then they could flip the point over, and direct their next strike with the small cobblestone to get a larger flake that would thin more to the middle of the point rather than the edge.

Wind supported the large flake on his left thigh on a scrap of soft leather. He struck with a downward motion, taking a flake off the lower side of the blade. He took several flakes along one edge, then ground the edge, flipped the point, and worked the other side.

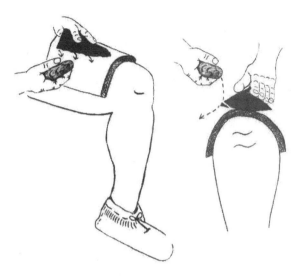

After looking at the stone from all angles, Wind planned the progression of his flakes, preparing the next strike. Spinning and turning the blade as he worked, thinning all edges until they were fairly straight and approximately in the center thickness of each edge of the stone. Wind was so skilled he made the process look easy. Once the blade had been thinned, he shaped it with a point at each end. It was as long as Wind's hand, about the thickness of his little finger at the center and tapered down to a knife's edge on the sides.

Finally, he ground both edges lightly, then went over them again, popping off fine flakes with just the pressure his hands could create using a fine-tipped deer antler. This time, he folded up a small scrap of buckskin and placed it in the palm of his left hand and laid the blade on it. He closed his fingers, effectively clamping the blade loosely in his hand. He then took small flakes as he had done the large ones, only rather than striking the edge of the blade, he put pressure with the tip of the antler into the blade's ground edge and popped the flake off the lower edge into his palm, which was pro-tected by the folded leather. He told Boy to clean the flakes out of the leather pad after each was snapped off. It was too easy to drive a loose flake through the leather and cut his palm if he let flakes build up as he worked.

Point of knife at thick end of spall

Handle of knife at thin end of spall

His finished product was a beautiful black shiny knife similar to what Boy's knife must have looked like before it was broken.

Wind in the Grass first had Boy try pressure flaking on a couple of smaller flakes that had come off the knife he had made. Once Boy started getting the feel of it, Wind had Boy sharpen the good edge of his own knife. It had dulled through the year. Boy learned pressure flaking quickly. The percussion flaking with the elk antler billet did not come so easily.

Wind spalled up the rest of the obsidian nodule, and then let Boy grind and thin the larger flakes. He broke most of them in half.

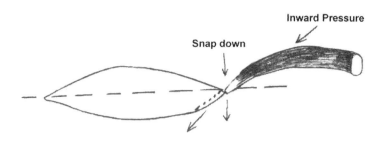

Others he narrowed down without getting them as thin as he should. He was frustrated with his performance. Wind had made it all look so easy! Wind kept correcting Boy's attempts by readjusting the angle he was holding the stone, or insuring that the boy gave it proper support. Not too tight, which would cause the energy of the strike to follow his fingers and break the blade. Not too loose, where the blade would move too much out of angle with the strike. When Boy had reduced the larger pieces to rubble, he wanted more, but he had brought back only the one nodule.

Wind taught him to make arrowheads out of the smaller flakes. Boy was not sure why he was making arrowheads but Wind cherished each one, and stored it in a little leather bag he made out of some of the buckskin. Finally, on a clear dry day, boy decided to go see if he could get another nodule. Taking his short spear to dig through the snow, he was sure he could find the hillside where he had gathered the obsidian before, but he would have to dig to find the obsidian vein. Laughing Wolf followed him. Wind asked him to look for the plant that grew long, straight stalks covered with sharp points that looked like little bear claws. They would have little round bulbs, the remains of flowers that Fire Woman might have used to make tea. Boy said he'd look for them.

Boy returned just at sundown. He was wet and cold, but wore a large grin. He had found the obsidian vein and managed to dig

through the snow and pry loose two large nodules. One he had carried under an arm while the other he drug over the snow using his
carry bag as a sled. This second one was much bigger than he probably could have carried in summer but the snow helped him get it back
to the cave. With Wind's help, he put them inside, then sat down
next to the fire to warm himself. He told Wind that about halfway to
where he found the rock, he had found a large patch of the sticker
bushes that Wind had asked about. He broke off a twig and put it in
the bottom of his carry bag to make sure it was what Wind wanted. It
was.

Wind told him that if he went out again in that direction, he
should cut as many as he has fingers on both hands. They should be
as tall as Boy's shoulders and the thick end should be about as big
around as Wind's longest finger. He would have to scrape a spot to

166 | KIRBY RECORDS

hold the shoot so it would not poke him. Then he would cut it loose and scrape off the rest of the little claws so he could pack it home. Boy promised to do what he could.

Now that Boy had flint knapping material to work with, Wind taught him how to examine the large nodule and figure where to strike it with the hammer stone to get the best spall. He taught Boy how to read the rock and follow with another strike to get the most out of the nodule. He had Boy break all of both nodules into spalls. Each spall was shaped using percussion flaking but only roughly. About the time they were starting to look good, Wind took them away and had Boy start on the next spall. By the time all the spalls were roughed into blade blanks, Boy was doing really well at the thinning process.

Now Wind let him start with the thickest of the rough blades, and taught him the ways of reading the rock and grinding the edges to set up his next strikes. Boy began thinning the blades even more while maintaining the width. Wind made Boy go through all of his rough blades this way. Boy broke considerably fewer than the first nodule he had tried. Wind figured the work involved in getting these two nodules had made the boy think twice and listen closer to what he was trying to teach him. Once Boy was through with his second thinning and shaping, Wind had him finish his first knife. It was as long as Boy's hand and a little over half as wide. It was thicker than Wind's knife, but it was straight and had a fine, serrated, sharp edge.

Boy was quite proud of his new blade. He immediately replaced his old knife with the new one. Wind suggested that Boy save the roughed out blades in the back of the cave to finish later, but Boy had to work one more knife just because he was so pleased with the first. This one he would leave under his sleeping shelf as a back up to the one he would pack with him daily.

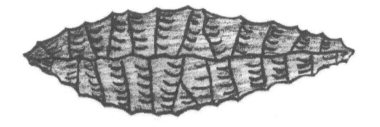

CHAPTER NINETEEN

Winter Projects

It was several weeks after making his stone knives that Boy left the cave to retrieve the sticker bush shoots for Wind in the Grass. Wind asked him to gather the yellow sticky blood of the trees that stayed green all winter. He said to look for places the trees had been wounded and they would have their yellow blood built up like the scabs red blood makes on our skin. He told Boy to use a stick to pick it off the tree because it would stick to his hands and be hard to clean. Wind sent with him another small leather bag he had prepared for this purpose, to prevent the sticky pitch from getting all over the inside of Boy's carry bag.

Boy utilized his new knife well. Wind had shown him how to use a leather scrap to wrap one end of the blade while he used the other. Then he could swap ends when the first end became dull.

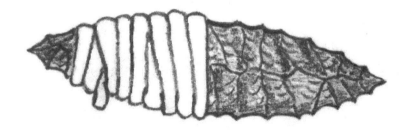

He also had Boy pack a small deer antler tine with him so he could sharpen his blade if needed. Boy took all day and returned with a few more shoots than the old man had asked for, just to make sure he had enough of the right size. Wind finished scraping each one, peeling off all the inner bark. He sorted out about four that were too thin or had a defect that would not allow him to make a proper arrow. Those he set aside for other uses, tied up his bundled shafts tightly, and placed them in the dry back of the cave away from the fire. Every day he unbundled them and bent them as needed across the palm of his left hand. Looking down the length of each one, he checked its straightness. The first couple of days they seemed to bend back to their original curves, but on the third day they began to stay straight. And ten days later, they were quite straight. Wind set them away for another ten days to cure, but they would stay straight now tied up in the bundle.

Wind in the Grass started a new project. He used a fist-sized hard rock and began tapping on a larger rock that sat flat on the cave floor. It was the rock that Boy had first used to push water to Mother Wolf. A little at a time, indentation of the rock was crumbling away, leaving **it** deeper. The bowl formed slowly, but surely, and when Wind didn't work on it, he had Boy work on it. Within a few days, they had made what Wind was calling his glue pot. He set it close to the fire, flat on the floor and with the indentation on top. He leaned a flat rock out over the coals from the edge of his bowl. Once the flat rock was heating up, Wind let the fire burn down to just coals. He put some of the yellow pine pitch on the flat rock and as it heated up next to the fire, the pitch began to melt. The melted pitch ran down the flat rock and dripped into the glue pot. Wind warned Boy that this process must be done with no open flames because the pitch could catch fire and it would burn far too hot and bright to handle.

Next, Wind ground up black ash from a mostly burnt stick and mixed it into the melting pitch. He said it would be better if they had some small fibers to mix in, but it would have to work for now. Wind removed the glue pot from the coals and then began twisting a stick in the glue. It built up on the stick in a glob until most of the glue was on the stick rather than in the pot. Once it grew to the diameter of his largest finger, Wind dunked it in the cold water of the drinking pool. He pulled it out and quickly shaped it and dunked it again, holding it under water long enough to cool. He repeated the process for a second glue stick, then set them and the glue pot aside for later.

When Wind was satisfied the arrow shafts were dried enough, he sorted through them again. Some had split too much to be of use, so he rejected those shafts. He then cut each shaft shorter, picking the straightest part of the shaft. He determined an arrow's length by making them as long as from his shoulder to his fingertip, then adding the length of his hand to that measurement. He cut the first one, and used it to measure the rest. Once he had cut all the shafts to the proper length, he scraped each one carefully to remove natural thick spots and to make them even straighter than they had been. He was also thinning the shafts so that they all had about the same diameter at the wider tip end and all had a consistent diameter at the narrower string end. Before he completed this stage he had discarded two more shafts that were weak and bent too easily. He wanted all of them to be as close to the same bending strength as he could get them.

With a flake of obsidian Wind made a special point that was about as long as the first joint of his finger. He made it as narrow as he could get it, except for the back end that flared out flat with notches to mount into a shaft. Trimming one of the discarded arrow shafts to about the length of his forearm, he then cut a slit in one end. On this slit he melted a small bit of the glue from the stick he had made earlier, heating the glue on the end of the stick over coals until it was soft. Then he fastened the new point into it and tied it in with wet sinew, tightening the sinew into the soft glue and warming the glue as needed to finish. He dunked the tip into water to cool the glue, then smoothed it out with his fingers.

Earlier Wind had made a small hand drill. He put the point on a piece of wood, and spun the shaft back and forth between his hands, causing the point to drill a hole in the wood.

He drilled each narrow end of the shafts with two holes across from each other and about half of one finger's width back from the end. Then using an obsidian flake, he split the shaft twice down from the end to each side of the holes. This allowed him to pop out the center of the shaft, leaving a perfect notch to fit over a bow string. Then using a flake, he scraped the notch smooth around the edges.

He repeated the process at the opposite end. This time the notch he was creating was three times as deep. When he finished notching the point end, he matched an arrowhead with a shaft and carved out the notch to fit the arrowhead so it would spin straight. He attached each point with the pitch glue and sinew. After the glue cooled, he rounded, tapered, and smoothed the end of the shaft that was lapped over each side of the arrowhead. This would keep the point from hanging up on the skin of an animal as it struck. He did this process for each shaft and tested each one to make sure it spun on its point without wobbling. He had to heat up the glue on a couple and re-straighten the arrowhead to get the wobble out of them when they had shifted before the glue dried.

When he was done, he had four arrows with obsidian arrow-heads and two shafts left without points. On these two arrows, he made a small game blunt. He strengthened the tips by wrapping them in sinew and melting glue over that. He could shoot these arrows over and over without worrying that a point might break.

All he needed to complete his arrows was feathers. The feathers would be attached in front of the bowstring notch to catch the wind and make the arrow shoot straight. He bundled the shafts again and set them in the back of the cave until he could finish them.

Finding feathers was an issue. Normally they would be gathered in the spring near a lake or river when the water birds were molting. There might be a chance to find some big enough feathers if an owl or hawk died and Boy would happen upon the carcass, but that was a long shot. The primary wing feathers of geese or turkey were the best, though others could be used. He told Boy what he needed. Boy said he would try to find some.

Another skill Wind taught Boy was making string from the plant stalks of stinging nettles. He asked if Boy had seen these plants last summer. The boy remembered the patch he had walked around the day he had discovered the glassy obsidian rock. Wind asked him to pick as many of the dried stalks as he could carry. They would not sting him now that the leaves had fallen. When Boy brought what stalks he could find back to the cave, Wind put several in the stream below the drinking hole. After a while he started pulling them out of the water and rolling them vigorously between his hands. They crumbled, revealing long fibers within the stalks. Carefully he removed any woody pieces clinging to the fibers. Once Boy amassed a pile of fibers, Wind showed him how to twist them into a string, how to add fibers to the twisting process, and how to keep an eye on the diameter of the string to keep the thickness consistent. Putting this new skill into practice, Boy made a ball of string. Wind in the Grass also made a ball of string. It was very handy when traveling.

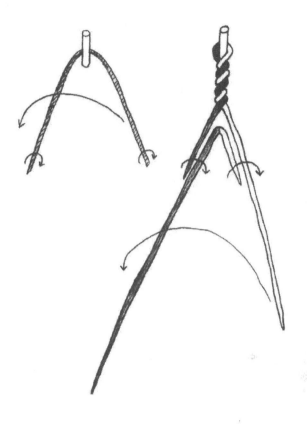

CHAPTER TWENTY

Winter Hunting

During the storms of midwinter the wolves spent most of their time in the cave. Boy rationed the dried meat to make sure it held out as long as possible. The wood did not last as long, so when there was a lull in the weather, Boy gathered firewood. There were always small sticks under the limbs of the larger trees. Logs were buried under the snow until he found one freshly blown down on top of the snow. He packed the larger limbs back and stocked up on these when he could.

Mother was nervous and paced back and forth, but she knew how tired she would get traveling on three legs in the deep snow. Boy and Laughing Wolf wrestled and played, much to the amusement of Wind. Mother seemed to enjoy the show too. Laughing Wolf didn't look much like a pup anymore. Now that he outweighed Boy, he could easily overpower him, but he never played mean. He considered Boy as a sibling, an equal. They both showed reverence to Mother. As far as Laughing Wolf was concerned, she was the leader of the pack. And both wolves showed reverence to Boy, who was not the pack leader, but could to do many things the wolves couldn't. They respected him for that. Mother saw the human as another cub that needed to be trained. She just didn't know quite how to do it!

Wind in the Grass was ignored by the wolves but accepted as a friendly outsider because the boy accepted him.

Wind saw his responsibility as the ongoing education of Boy. He told the boy his stories of life experiences. Each story was designed to teach a point on survival, hunting, or dealing with people. Boy was thankful for these stories. He listened closely and did not interrupt the old man's recollections, but peppered Wind with questions afterward. Some of the stories included songs. Wind sang and tapped his hand on his leg to sound like a drum. Over the winter months, Boy learned several songs and sang with Wind.

When the winter turned really cold, the snow crusted over. The wolves could get out easier now. The crusted snow supported their weight spread out over their large feet. They were naturally equipped to run about in the cold with their heavy fur. Laughing Wolf soon discovered that the deer could not run as fast in the deep snow. The deer kept specific trails packed down and tried to stay on those trails, but if the wolf scared one off its trail, it broke through the snow and sank to its belly. Laughing Wolf began making a kill by himself now and then. The wolves liked the tender innards and ate them first. They left the meat of the hips for Boy. In the cold, the meat could be left outside the cave where it froze and kept well. Laughing Wolf relished in this boon to his hunting success and killed frequently. Mother thought it was a little too frequently, but they were hunting for four, and Boy seemed to make a lot of useful things from each kill.

When boy noticed blood on Laughing Wolf's fur, he would backtrack and find the kill. Wind in the Grass told him how to salvage the long sinew along each side of the deer's back. He told boy how to skin out the hide to get the best use of it when tanning it.

Wind had Boy bring back the head so the skull could be broken open and the brains used for tanning hides. He taught Boy how to cut out leg sinew and how to dry it for later pounding. Some hides were stretched flat to dry in a frame made of poles. Boy had brought the poles in for firewood, but Wind had used four of them to make a hide frame. These flat hides were left with the hair on and some were used as sleeping mats on the cave's cold, dirt floor.

Even with only three legs to work with, Mother couldn't remember a more comfortable winter. She was more used to long periods of starving and very colds nights spent out in the weather. She thought the boy was a useful addition to her pack.

Wind in the Grass' health improved as the winter progressed. His leg was mostly healed and although it was not as mobile as a human leg should be, he could put some weight on it now. He walked with a heavy limp and used his walking stick for balance. He knew if he made it back to his clan, his days as a scout were over. Still, he thought about getting back to where younger hunters and warriors would be protecting the tribe.

He felt safe in the cave knowing the enemy would be at their winter camps and not venturing out in the deep snow. But he knew spring would bring the enemy back to the far reaches of their territory and he could not defend the boy as he had before. He decided that when the snow melted, he would offer to take the boy south to try to intercept his people on their northward journey.

Wind told stories about his people, his own father, and the honors the tribe had bestowed on him. He shared stories of his personal heroes, those he had looked up to while growing up. Stories of some of the young people he knew that would be about Boy's age. He was raising the boy's interest in his own people.

Spring came late that year. The group had fared well over the winter. With the fresh deer kills and all the dried meat, they had not gone hungry. As the snow melted, Laughing Wolf found deer were now harder to catch and his ability to make a kill declined. They ate dried meat again when fresh was not available. Wood was getting easier to find, but now was farther to pack. Boy had used up all the wood within walking distance. The days were wet and the wind was cold, so they spent a lot of time in the cave by the fire. Even Mother thought the fire was a good thing now.

The winter kills had yielded enough buckskin and brains that Wind had outfitted both himself and boy with new leggings, breechcloth, and long shirt that would not only be comfortable for the foreseeable future but were also presentable to the tribe should they reach it. He had made three pairs of moccasins for each of them as well.

Now that he could get out and move about, he went walking to strengthen his leg. It still hurt now and again, and he still used his walking staff for balance, but he was moving about better. He figured he would never walk the same as he had before the bear had attacked him.

Wind limped along the high ridges looking for the right type of tree to make a new bow. When he finally found one, it took him most of the day to cut a stave. The stave had to be longer than the finished bow and about the right width but as thick as the finished handle would be. Staves were cut from thick patches of hardwood, where the lack of room made the tree stretch tall to try to reach the light. These small trees had fewer limbs, tighter growth rings, and were straighter than normal growth hardwood.

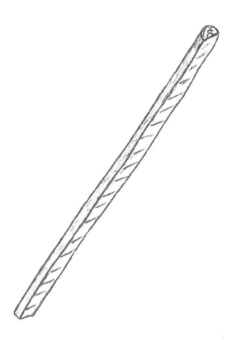

Wind returned to the cave after dark, and was disappointed he had found only one stave. He knew he could do better next time. He made several trips and cut a total of three staves. He wanted to make a bow and arrows for both him and the boy. They may need them when traveling. He used the hand axe to flatten out one side of the first stave. Next he carefully carved the edges into his favorite flat bow design. He also smoothed and rounded the handle so it was comfortable in his hand.

After the bow was shaped, he carefully started scraping the

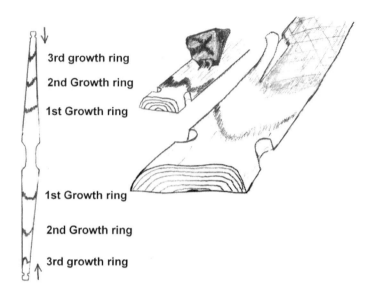

3rd growth ring

2nd Growth ring

1st Growth ring

1st Growth ring

2nd Growth ring

3rd growth ring

back, starting at one end toward the middle. He had chosen a growth ring three layers down and was scraping down to that layer but not through it. Working from both ends, he removed small shavings of wood from the back of the bow. He followed the chosen growth ring up the stave until the whole bow was a single smooth layer of wood. This was necessary to prevent the finished bow from splitting.

Once the back was scraped and the bow shaped and smooth, Wind held the upper end in his hand and rested the lower end on a piece of leather on the ground. He pressed down on the handle of the stave, testing the bend of both limbs of the bow. It was barely flexing. Using a sharp shard of stone, he scraped the side of the bow that would face him when the bow was ready to shoot. He took just a small amount of scrapings off the belly of the bow before testing the bend of the limbs again. He paid attention to stiff spots as he scraped and tested, working the limbs into an even arc.

As soon as it was flexing evenly with just enough bend, he made a bow string out of twisted marmot rawhide. He carved the tips of each limb to hold the string and strung the roughed-out bow with just a hint of flex in the wood. This way he could bend the bow slightly and check for stiffness. Wind continued to scrape wood off the belly of the bow leaving the back alone, being careful not to damage the growth ring he had carefully isolated.

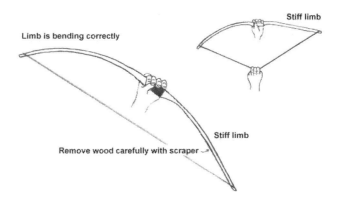

Stiff limb

Limb is bending correctly

Stiff limb

Remove wood carefully with scraper

He "tillered" the bow by flexing it and noting stiff spots in each limb. Then he scraped those areas, taking just enough wood off the belly to eliminate the stiffness.

Wind checked his progress frequently to prevent taking too much wood, which might allow a limb to bend too much. As the bow bent more, he shortened the string. When he had the string the right length, he could make a fist with his thumb sticking up, and place it between the bow handle and the string. The string was just above the tip of his thumb. At this point, he just needed to get the bow to flex enough for him to pull it back as far as his arms allowed. Wind was trying to keep as much strength in the bow as possible. Once the bow was shaped and drawing back in a "D" shaped arc, nearly to his full draw length, he stopped scraping.

Now Wind prepared to cover the back of his bow with sinew to give it more strength and prevent breaking. He mixed small rawhide scrapings with water and boiled them into hide glue. He hammered out sinew strips and shredded them into strands. When he had enough glue heated, he coated the back of his bow and pressed glue-soaked sinew strands onto it. He made one complete layer starting at the tips and working back to the handle. Setting the bow aside to dry, he prepared the second layer. Once the first layer was dry to the touch, he applied the next, finishing with a third layer. The last layer was placed more centered on the bow so the glue and sinew tapered to the edges.

He re-tillered the belly of the bow to reach his draw length. The final draw length was determined by his arrow length. Draw length was shorter than arrow length because the stone point needed to be out in front of his hand when he pulled the arrow back to shoot. Draw length was the distance he would pull the string back each time so that he would have consistent energy transfer to the arrow when released. Wind brought the arrow back to where his top finger on the string, touched the corner of his mouth allowing him to sight down the arrow for better accuracy.

The dried sinew had added considerable strength to the pull of the bow, and would keep the back from cracking under stress. The final belly scraping was really fine to make a smooth finish. Using a scrap of buckskin, he rubbed down the bow with rendered fat to keep water from penetrating the wood. He repeated this rubbing over a period of several days until he had a reliably water-resistant finish. He admired his work. It was a carefully crafted bow that would handle either hunting or warring. He made a second string for the bow in case the first one broke.

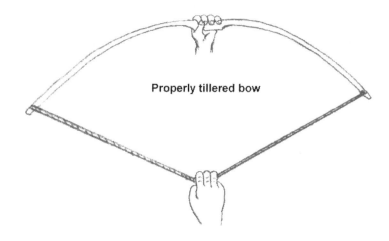

Properly tillered bow

Wind in the Grass then slid his new bow into the case where he had kept his old bow until the day it was broken in the river. He figured he may not move about as well as he once did, but he could still shoot a bow accurately. He wanted to finish the arrows he had started, but he didn't have the feathers he needed.

Wind in the Grass started a second bow for Boy. This one was shorter and not as strong. It took every bit as much care to build and nearly as much time. He told Boy he should never let loose of the string at full draw without an arrow on it. The bow needed the weight of the arrow to transfer its energy. Mistreatment of a bow could cause it to break. He should never leave it strung when not hunting because the tension of the string on the bow would cause the bow to lose some of its power over time. Just like Boy needed rest after a day's work, so did the bow. When not using the bow, he should keep the bow in a case up off the damp ground. Dampness could seep into the wood and cause it to weaken. This is why Wind kept his bow greased with the fat of a kill. Wind made a quiver and case for Boy's new bow using soft, tanned doe hide. The third bow stave he hung in the back of the cave to stay dry. It would be ready to make into a bow should the need arise.

CHAPTER TWENTY ONE

Heading South

Wind in the Grass was getting restless. He wanted to head south and take Boy with him. Boy was ready to travel too. One morning on a sunny day, Wind got up early and began packing the important things he would need. He couldn't travel as lightly as he was used to because he would have the boy with him. He also was not as mobile as he had been last fall when he had arrived. He packed dried meat, his robe, his bow, and partially built arrows. He packed the dried long sinews he had taught Boy to cut from the back of the deer that Laughing Wolf had killed. He packed his extra moccasins, and a small buckskin bag of arrowheads he had chipped out of the shiny rock Boy had found. All this he rolled up in his sleeping robe and tied with a strap that could be slung over his shoulder. Then he could put his bow case and quiver over that. He would walk with his walking stick for balance. Last he placed his war axe and knife on a belt at his side where he could reach them quickly.

He knew the enemy would be restless too. They may come looking for the warriors who didn't make it back last fall to see what had happened to them. If they found their remains they would know it was no accident and they would be interested in exacting revenge on anyone not of their people.

Wind helped Boy pack his gear as Laughing Wolf and Mother looked on. Boy packed his fire board and drill, his spool of string, his cat claws, and two knives into his gathering pouch with some dried meat. He packed his extra moccasins with more dried meat, then rolled them up in his fur sleeping robe. He tied off the sleeping robe like Wind had done and slung this over his shoulder. He also slung on the bow case and bow Wind had made him. His arrows were unfinished, straightened shafts, but Wind assured him they would complete some arrows along the way. Boy left his fish spear in the back of the cave. They would not need it on the journey, and he could always make another now that he knew how. Boy did pack his short spear. It still had the blood stain of the big cat. He trusted that spear as his best weapon. He had not yet learned to shoot his bow.

What was left in terms of hides, food, useable stones, and baskets, was placed in the nearly empty storage holes and covered with the rock lids. The stash would be there as a backup should they need to return.

The sun was up and warming when the four companions left the cave. Boy looked back with a bit of sadness as he crested the top of the ridge. He knew this was no ordinary hunting trip. He wondered if he would ever return. It was a place of learning and wonderful memories, but was also a place of loss and sad memories. He turned south and set his mind to the adventure ahead of him.

They made decent progress that day, getting well beyond the sight of his first deer kill. Wind had a distinctive limp and Boy could tell his leg was weak, if not hurting. Although the weather was mild, snow still lingered on the northern sides of ridges and in the deep timber where the sun did not visit much. The ground was soft and damp so they would get cold when they stopped to rest Wind's leg. Just before dark they found a place sheltered from the wind to set up camp. Boy started the fire, this time using his hand drill and fireboard as Wind had taught him. They sat between downed rocks and fallen trees. The fire's heat reflected off both surfaces and warmed them. They ate a small portion of their dried meat. They would protect that resource as best as they could because they did not know how long before fresh food would be available.

Mother and Laughing Wolf had kept the men within eyesight but traveled away from them, exploring the territory in a circle around the men as they moved through the day. This was familiar territory for the wolves just as it had been for Wind in the Grass. They had traveled this country on their hunting trips and had gone even farther out onto the plains when Mother had been training Laughing Wolf.

Mother sensed the men meant to travel far this time. Laughing Wolf was thinking it was just another outing to find hunting opportunities. He was laughing at the prospect as usual.

The next day was similar to the first. Snow hid on the shaded sides of trees and boulders. The snow had to be crossed in places, but the ground was bare where the sun spent most of its time during the day. The slipperiness of the snowy areas made it hard on Wind's legs and back as he had to work hard to keep his balance. The elevation began to drop, and they walked out to a point above a series of benches formed by short cliffs of volcanic rock. They could see out over the great expanse of these benches down to a prairie below. Wind in the Grass stood on this point for a long time studying the route they would take. He pointed out the lower reaches of the river that had run by the cave. Now it was a shiny ribbon leading to a lake out on the flatness below. He pointed out the ridges on the western end of the prairie where they would walk to try to find Wind in the Grass' people. It would be a long walk, he told Boy, and there could be encounters with other people, friendly or not. Boy looked forward to the adventure.

It was on this point, as the travelers looked to their route that Mother's original pack finally caught up with her.

CHAPTER TWENTY TWO

Separate Ways

The pack was hunting on the next bench below the point and had a doe on the run. The sounds of the moving hunters caught all of the travelers' attention at once. They watched, intrigued by the coordinated attack as the wolf hunters took turns running the old doe and tiring her while keeping the pack well rested. As they came closer, Laughing Wolf could not help but dive into the chase. This was something he knew. He was up for a hunt. Mother followed him off the point and down to the next flat, but for a different reason. She knew he was in danger. He knew the hunt, but he did not know the rules of a pack, and they might well kill him if he was not subordinate to the pack leader and his mate.

Laughing Wolf took advantage of his angle of attack, unexpected as it was, by the deer or the other hunters. He plowed into the doe at such a high rate of speed that it sent her sprawling. The other hunters were on her in a flash and ripped into the deer as ravenous killers. They had not eaten as well through the winter as Laughing Wolf had. The pup's alliance to the men had kept him fed in the lean times. Mother arrived behind Laughing Wolf and headed him off from dashing into the kill with the others. They were quickly surrounded by the rest of the pack. The lead wolf approached Mother and she lowered her head. Laughing Wolf did not. The lead wolf attacked Laughing Wolf, viciously ripping his skin at the shoulder. Laughing Wolf yelped and spun, but the big wolf kept up the attack. Mother growled and snapped at the leader. Then forcing herself between him and her pup, she bit Laughing Wolf on the neck as hard as she had ever done. Laughing Wolf was confused. Mother had never done this before! His confusion gave the leader enough of an advantage to knock Laughing Wolf down and grab his throat. Laughing Wolf stopped fighting and went limp. Mother growled at the leader, who then released his grip on Laughing Wolf but stood over him with his sharp teeth close enough to grab him again.

The leader recognized Mother. She had once been the mate to a previous leader who had been killed in a fight with a bear. This female had been wounded. The pack had given her up for dead. He had fought to become the new leader, and he and his mate now ruled the pack. Yet there was some respect owed to a past leader, as long as she understood her place now. The big wolf he stood over was obviously young, male, and a well-trained hunter. The lead wolf did not want to kill such an asset, if he would join the pack, but he had to know his place. The pack leader stood by as each of the other wolves came and engaged Laughing Wolf in a fight. Laughing Wolf had learned the lesson and let each one take him down. He showed the older hunters the respect they demanded, and when the ordeal was through, the pecking order was reinforced when the leaders fed first.

Mother stood with Laughing Wolf and the two of them fed only after all the others wolves had eaten. As night fell, the pack headed off to the west. The pack had two members more than they had started with that morning.

From his vantage point, Boy had witnessed the attack. He was going to charge in to protect his brother from the pack, but Wind in the Grass stopped him. They watched together, and Wind explained how the wolves were just making sure Laughing Wolf understood respect for his elders. If he would stop fighting them, he would most likely be accepted. Besides, if Boy were to charge in to the fray, the pack would see the human as a lone enemy and attack him. There was nothing to do but watch. It was as emotionally painful for Boy to watch as it was for Laughing Wolf to experience. When it was over, Boy was relieved Laughing Wolf was alive, but was devastated when Mother and Laughing Wolf left with the pack. Wind tried to explain that they were traveling to his tribe and that it was only right for the wolves to join back with their pack as well. Still, the wolves had been Boy's only companions until Wind had come along. He considered them his family, or at least he was part of their pack. To keep the boy's mind occupied, Wind started him traveling again.

Wind was thinking this was a good thing. It might be hard to walk back into an encampment followed by two wolves without his warriors killing the wolves before he had a chance to explain the situation. If the wolves joined their pack, they would not follow the men all the way across the prairie. They worked their way around the cliffs and down to the river.

That night boy slept restlessly. He had nightmares of being left alone again.

Wind was having a rough night too. Something was bothering him and he wasn't sure what it was. He felt uneasy, but figured it was just in knowing that a wolf pack was out there close by and hunting. His awareness skills had suffered in the cave all winter. They were returning now.

The next day, Wind and Boy followed the river south and along the edge of the plain. They saw no sign of the wolves all day. Edible plants were available, so Wind and Boy ate fresh greens as they moved. It was a good change from the winter long meat diet. The weather remained pleasant, and they covered a lot of ground in spite of Wind's stiff leg. They followed the river as it wound toward the lake.

The boy and old man traveled well together, discussing what they saw, what plants or bones they encountered could be used for, what tracks they found might tell them. Boy saw new animals, like the antelope which were skinnier than the deer he had hunted and much faster. They did not let the travelers get very close. Then there were the rabbits—lots of rabbits! Boy thought he could trap a few if they had time, but they kept walking. Ground squirrels were everywhere too, and the snakes that hunted them. Wind pointed out the poisonous snakes.

"You need to learn those well," he said, pointing to a poisonous snake. "They can kill you." Wind was good at spotting and avoiding them.

They had traveled three more days after Mother and Laughing Wolf had left with the wolf pack when Boy heard what sounded like a lot of people laughing. He asked Wind if that was his people ahead. It was not. As they crested a little rise, Boy saw before him a huge body of water. It was the lake they had seen from above, only it was much bigger than it had appeared from up there. Wind pointed out the geese on the lake.

"Look!" he said "we can gather some feathers."

The big water birds lose their feathers in the spring and grow new ones.

"We can find enough goose feathers along the shore for our arrows," Wind said.

They began gathering the larger wing feathers they found on the ground near the lake. They gathered many feathers. Wind showed Boy how some feathers came from a bird's right wing and some came from the left. He could tell by the curve of the feather itself. Also he showed how the upward side of the feather was shinier than the bottom. He told Boy that when putting feathers on the arrow, they needed to all be aligned with the shiny sides all one direction and the feather angled back towards the string. They gathered feathers as they walked along the shore. When Wind was sure they had enough feathers for the arrow shafts, they turned from the lake following a small stream back towards the foothills along the western edge of the prairie. They followed the stream to a large grove of cottonwood trees where they could make a sheltered camp.

The cottonwood patch was between the river and an abrupt rise to the foothills west of their line of travel. It afforded some protection from the weather. They set up camp and decided to stay a few days, long enough to try to catch some fish and complete their arrows. Wind thought it would be a good rabbit hunting area to teach

Boy how to shoot his bow. Food was plentiful, and he wanted to rest his recovering leg before traveling again.

Wind walked with Boy along the creek a short distance, then pointed out a rather large trout resting in the shallows just under the edge of the opposite stream bank. He told Boy to wait there and keep an eye on the fish. Wind then went back down the small stream a short distance and jumped across it. When he arrived across from Boy, he asked the exact location of the fish. Boy pointed to it. Wind in the Grass lay down on the bank and slipped his hand in the water behind the fish ever so slowly. Then, just as slowly, he moved his hand upstream under the fish, gently stroking its belly. Once he had reached the fishes' front fins, he quickly but gently lifted the fish up and out of the water! It was as if the fish didn't care if Wind took him. Boy was amazed. Wind had Boy try. They moved along the banks and Wind pointed to a fish. Boy tried several times, but always moved too quickly, spooking the fish. Finally, Boy was able to slow down his movements enough to pull a fish from the water with his hands. Once they had two fish, they headed back to camp to cook dinner.

As the sun went down, Wind began preparing feathers. He grabbed the upper small end of the quill with his left hand and the right side of the feathers with his right hand. He carefully pulled, keeping steady pressure on the feather until it began to separate from the quill. He then kept pressure while pulling the feather away from the quill until the feather came loose all the way down to the lower end, the thickest part of the quill. He did this with all the feathers. He separated them into two piles: those with the shiny left side and those with the shiny right side.

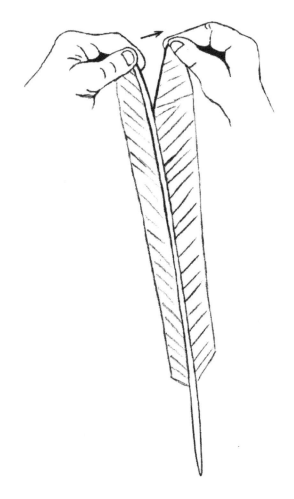

Picking three feathers from one pile, he trimmed them to an equal length. He pulled out the dried strip of back sinew he had brought and began pounding it, separating it into thin threads. He peeled off one of these thin long threads. He chewed on the sinew to soften it and let it form its own glue.

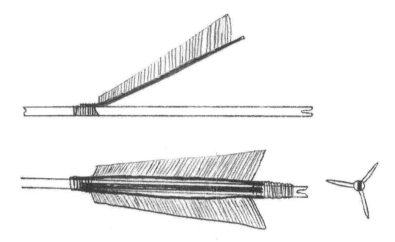

Lining up the first feather perpendicular to the string slot at the end of the arrow, he set it on straight with the shaft and slightly forward of the base of the knock. He wrapped the sinew around the arrow shaft and across the feather's front end. Then adding another feather, he took two more wraps before adding a third. He spaced the feathers equal distance around the shaft. He used the full length of the sinew thread and covered the ends of the feather well. He then tied the upper end, spacing the feathers to line up straight with the shaft. Starting a finger's width down the feather quill, he wrapped up the arrow shaft to just under the knock. This held the upper part of the feather and reinforced the knocking slot. He adjusted the feathers once more before he was done. He did this for all the shafts he had straightened last winter—those he now carried and those Boy carried. Some arrows had feathers with shiny left sides and some had shiny right sides, but all three feathers on one arrow were always the same.

He gave Boy the shafts without points. He said they would kill a rabbit if you took out both lungs, or hit him square in the head. The best part was that without a stone tip, they could be shot over and over with less breakage. Boy put them in his quiver. Tomorrow he would try his hand at hunting rabbits with a bow. Wind finished up the rest of his arrows, some with stone arrowheads. They might come in handy if they encountered an enemy.

Wind showed Boy how to hold his bow properly and how to set an arrow on the string in a straight line with the knuckles on his bow hand. To hold the string and arrow at the same time, Wind had Boy put one finger above the arrow and two below, leaving his small finger and thumb loose. The string fit into the groove of skin just behind the fingertips of his three string fingers. Boy began to pull tension on the string. Wind told him to relax his grip on the string just enough to twist the arrow sideways against the bow. Boy pulled the string until his hand touched his face. Wind explained that it was important to pull the string back the same distance each time so it would deliver the same amount of energy to the arrow when released. Wind adjusted Boy's bow arm so that he held it slightly bent and the bow at an angle, creating a "V" between his knuckles and the side of his bow. Boy practiced until his consistency in shooting form developed into accuracy. Wind reminded Boy to watch his arrow fly with each shot. The arrow would tell him if it hit the animal, where it hit, and how hard. If it missed, it would tell him where to find it.

Boy discovered the prairie was not as flat as it had looked from above. It hid gullies, bogs, and other areas that he had to avoid. As Boy hunted rabbits and practiced fishing with his bare hands, Wind watched and made suggestions or asked the boy questions for which

Boy would have to search for the answers. At Wind's insistence, Boy caught several fish with his hands, but then let them go. He wanted to eat a rabbit tonight.

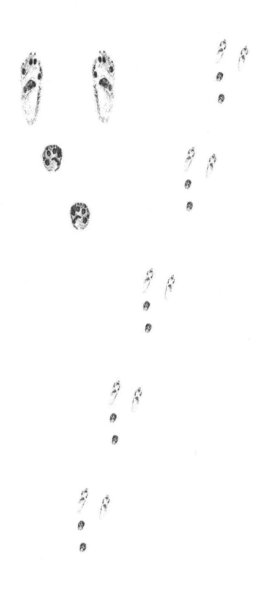

He spent the afternoon shooting his bow at rabbits, many times hitting close to his prey, but did not connect. Wind did not move about much. He mostly stayed in the shade and rested up for the next long walk of their journey. He watched and coached as Boy hunted in a circle around him. Wind coached him in proper shooting form and what to expect from the bow and arrow, where to aim on a rabbit for a clean kill, but he also coached Boy in stalking his prey. Boy finally made a kill when he moved slowly enough to get really close. His arrow penetrated the rib cage of a large male, taking out both lungs. Wind congratulated him and told him it would be the same for a deer or a large elk. Place that arrow through both lungs and the animal would die quickly and not suffer. Miss even one lung and he would be tracking the animal long after dark.

Wind announced to Boy that they would continue their journey in the morning. Wind made a small fire so they could cook the rabbit. They hung the rabbit hide on a tree limb to deal with in the morning. Boy eventually fell asleep after their usual discussion on life and plans. Lying on the opposite side of the fire from Boy, Wind drifted in and out of sleep. His mind was working through the events of the last few days and trying to figure out what was causing his uneasy feeling. He had a nagging feeling that something wasn't right. Then he heard it—the definitive sound. It was just a twig snapping. It could have been a coyote wandering in the night, but it wasn't.

CHAPTER TWENTY THREE

Battle!

The bear charged out of the night so quickly that Wind hardly had time to grab his war axe before the beast was upon him. He gave a war cry, mostly for Boy's sake, though he knew Boy was waking with the sound of the attack.

Boy woke with a start and instinctively grabbed his spear. As he rose he saw the huge shadow moving over Wind who was fighting with all his might. The bear had him by one arm and was shaking him vigorously. Boy's fear turned to the rage he had felt with the big cat. Screaming desperately, he ran up to the bear and drove his spear deep into its side. The bear turned on him, and with one backstroke of his huge paw, batted the boy back into the shadows under the cottonwood trees. Wind used the moment to spin out from under the bear and landed a blow with his war axe to the bear's skull. It was a glancing blow, peeling skin from in front of his left ear down over its eye. Blood gushed onto the bear's face, but Wind knew the blow was not lethal. He would need to crush the skull in order to bring down the bear.

Boy picked himself up and charged again. Grabbing his spear end, he yanked it hard and pulled it out of the side of the bear, which had turned his attention back to Wind.

Wind leapt to the side, avoiding the bear's lunge. Wind turned deathly calm as he always did in a crisis, but his wounded leg did not allow him the agility he would have liked in this situation. He swung his axe again and it sunk deep into the bear's front shoulder.

At the same time, the bear swung and batted Wind squarely in the chest. The blow sent him flying backwards into one of the large cottonwood trunks. His head hit with a sickening thud and his body went limp in a pile on the ground. The bear rose up on its hind legs, preparing to land all its weight on Wind's unconscious body. Just then, Boy launched his spear and sunk it deep into the bear's back, causing the bear to spin as it came down to face Boy. The bear took little time to charge toward the small human who had hurt him again.

The boy roared his defiance in the face of the bear's charge, but about the time he expected to die in the bear's jaws, he was knocked to the side by another animal that came flying past him into the face of the bear. It was a wolf and it was ripping at the bear's face while standing on one rear leg. Mother! Boy moved around the bear, but his spear was still in the bear's back, sticking up in the air too high for him to get a grip on it. He looked around and saw the war axe on the ground to the rear of the bear. He dove for it and rolled out of the way of the bear's shuffling feet.

The bear had a real fight going on now as Mother Wolf defended her cub! She was much quicker than the humans had been. Sinking her teeth into the bear's neck, she ripped his throat. The bear dropped its weight down on the wolf, trying to crush it. At the same time, Boy landed a blow to the back of the bear's lower rear leg, cutting clean through a tendon and causing its foot to go limp. The bear roared and spun, knocking Boy off his feet, but Boy rolled with the blow and came back up holding the axe. Mother was swinging from the bear's throat like a loose necklace, refusing to let go.

Then another wolf joined the fight! Laughing Wolf hit the bear from the side with all his weight, knocking it sideways. The young wolf jumped onto the bear's back, intending to grab for the back of its neck, but the bear wasn't going to give him the chance. It dropped one shoulder, causing Laughing Wolf's momentum to send him sprawling beyond the bear into the bushes.

Mother, being caught up in the bear's maneuver, fell off balance, and a bear paw ripped through her shoulder. Yelping in pain, she tried to spin out of the way, but was not quick enough. The bear landed on her with both front feet and bit the back of her neck. Her body went limp. Together, Boy and Laughing Wolf charged the bear. Boy had seen Mother go limp, and his rage compelled him to leap on the bear's back, grabbing his spear shank as he straddled the bloody fur. Laughing Wolf took a full frontal attack, catching the bear in the throat as it rose to turn on the boy. Laughing Wolf's attack was so vicious that the bear could not turn. Boy pulled his spear free as he dropped to the ground. Wind was just coming to consciousness as the boy hit the ground and rolled up next to him.

He yelled to Boy: "Take out his lungs! He cannot fight for long without air!"

Boy stood up. A determined calm overtook him—the same calm he had seen in Wind in the Grass when he was fighting earlier. While Laughing Wolf had the bear's full attention, Boy walked up to the bear's side, moved in really close, and launched his spear. The sharp point penetrated the bear's hide behind the ribs on its right side, traveled through both lungs, and poked out in front of his left front leg. Boy immediately saw the bear's stature drop. Laughing Wolf got a fresh hold on the bear's throat as its attention turned to trying to leave the fight. Boy backed off and picked up Wind's axe again. The bear was still trying to bite the wolf, but now blood was running from its nose and mouth. The bear collapsed on Laughing Wolf. Boy ran forward and landed the hardest blow he could on the bear's skull right behind the ear. That was the end. The bear quit moving. Laughing Wolf wiggled out from under the bear once he realized the bear was dead.

Wind in the Grass tried to stand, but the world began spinning. He crawled over next to the fire and added what he could reach in small branches. They would need light to check for wounds. Boy pulled his spear free of the bear, then brought the war axe over to Wind and laid it beside him.

Surprisingly, Wind's arm was not broken. It had many serious puncture wounds, but he was not losing a lot of blood. The muscles would need healing before he could fully use it, but at least the bones were intact. He also had a serious bump on the back of his head. Boy had gashes on both arms and across his chest where the bear had raked him with his sharp claws. These were bleeding, but Wind thought they would heal without stitches. Laughing Wolf seemed unharmed, though he was covered in the bear's blood. Boy rubbed him all over and did not find a sore spot or open wound—just his earlier shoulder wound from the pack leader, and that was now healing. They turned their attention to Mother.

She lay still where the bear had dropped her. The bear had crushed the spine behind her head. She had died instantly. She had done her part to save her human cub, but she had given her life in the fight. Boy burst into tears. He hadn't cried through all the tragedy that had befallen him in the last year, but this was too much. He held her head in his lap and petted it slowly as he sobbed. Laughing Wolf lay down next to his mother and whined. She would not be teaching him again.

CHAPTER TWENTY FOUR

Moving On

Morning didn't come quickly enough. When it was light enough to see, Wind in the Grass checked the tracks to better understand the battle. His body was stiff and sore, but at least his head was not spinning. He looked over the bear. Even through its new wounds, it showed the old scars it carried from many battles. He checked the left front paw. Sure enough, it was missing two claws. This was the same bear that had broken his leg last fall! This bear had killed humans before. Wind knew this as truth. He had seen it and felt it. It was good that the bear was dead. It had hunted them, and would have continued to hunt man had it succeeded in killing them. This bear had fought other bears and wolves too. In fact, during her life, Mother had known this bear well. It was the bear that had killed her mate, the bear that had made her leg useless, and the bear that had almost taken her life last year if it had not been for the generous human cub who nourished her back to health. She had entered the fight in full rage, rage at this animal that continued to try to kill her family. Wind in the Grass may not have known Mother's story, but in her tracks he read the intensity of her attack.

Backtracking the bear's approach, Wind found that the bear had been following their trail for some time. The bear had lain in the bushes up the hill during the day and waited for night to fall when he knew his nose would give him the advantage of the attack. This was an intelligent bear, mean and intent on doing harm to all it hated, and it seemed to hate everything.

Boy was stiff and sore too. His wounds had scabbed over and he moved carefully and deliberately so as not to cause them to break open again. He dug a shallow grave in the sandy soil under the cottonwood trees and laid Mother's body in it. He covered her and laid a large flat rock on her grave. If he passed here again, he would visit her spirit.

Boy gathered and packed his own things. He took the time to cut off two of the bear's larger claws. He would string one with his cougar claw and wear it as proudly. He would keep the other safe with the second cougar claw. He did not know why, but he knew it would be important someday.

Just then, Wind in the Grass approached and stated in a loud, clear voice as if he was addressing a large group of people: "This young man is now a warrior!" He was looking around as if a group of people were watching his actions. "This young man has earned honors in battle! This young man will now be known as 'Wolf Who Kills with a Spear.'"

Then he addressed the boy directly, but as loudly as he had been speaking before: "Wolf Who Kills with a Spear, the warrior bear was killed by your hand—with your spear and my axe. I believe this axe will serve you better than it has me!"

With that, Wind in the Grass handed him the war axe!

Boy was surprised by the honor and the gift of the axe, but—more than that—he realized just what had happened. He had been named! Tears filled his eyes again, but this time, they were tears of pride. He knew he was no longer a boy, but a man. He had earned a real name.

Wind in the Grass put his arm around the young warrior and said in a much quieter voice: "This name is a good name, but I hope an old friend might shorten it a bit or my tongue will get tired every day of our journey! With your permission I will call you just 'Spear' when we talk as friends."

The young warrior replied to his old friend: "Then 'Spear' I shall answer to!"

Laughing Wolf was moving around, but he was quiet, sad, and uncertain. Following Mother as he always did, he had left the pack, even though he had not wanted to leave all the excitement they generated. The other wolves had things to do and see, things that interested Laughing Wolf and allowed him to test his hunting skills in competition with others of his kind. Mother had been intent on leaving immediately. She had caught a scent she would never forget. It filled her with rage and fear, but she sensed she was needed. Laughing Wolf followed her as he always had, though lagging a bit and wondering why she chose to leave just then.

This morning, Laughing Wolf sat by the flat stone and watched as the two humans prepared their gear to continue their journey. When they finally were ready, they turned south. Laughing Wolf let out a long, soulful howl—a song of the great loneliness he was feeling. Wolf Who Kills with a Spear turned and looked at his friend, his brother. He understood that feeling. He too, had it in his heart. Laughing Wolf howled again. Off in the foothills, behind them, another long howl sounded. The leader howled once, and the others joined in. Laughing Wolf answered them again. Then he trotted off in their direction, but stopped and looked back at the boy with questioning eyes. Wolf Who Kills with a Spear kneeled. Laughing Wolf ran to him and the boy hugged the big wolf tightly. The boy looked deeply into his brother's eyes, then let him go. Turning, Laughing Wolf ran off into the hills to catch up with his pack.

Wind in the Grass began walking again, and Wolf Who Kills with a Spear followed. They had passed out of sight of the battle and moved a short distance beyond when a lonely howl filled the air. Looking back, they saw Laughing Wolf on the point where the pack had been. He was singing his good bye. The boy raised his spear in the air and returned his brother's cry with a lonely howl of his own. Laughing Wolf disappeared over the ridge. Wind knew he had named the young warrior well.

For several hours, the two men continued walking without talking much. Wind was sore and thinking about their journey. Spear already missed the wolf family he had lived with for the last year. His mind knew there was no going back. He looked forward to meeting Wind's friends, but he would grieve his loss for a long time.

The trail moved along the western edge of the prairie, hugging the foothills. They traveled for several days before finding the southern border of the prairie. Here a shallow canyon led them further south, but climbed in elevation. The trail was well marked in the canyon by the many people and animals who used this trail through the mountain pass. The trail switched back and forth at the steepest part, then they crested the ridge and started down again. Spear could see the valley floor stretching out in front of them. The prairie they had crossed was a high mountain plateau and the valley ahead was much lower in elevation than the prairie had been. The trail moved down to the side of a rough, fast-moving river swirling on and around large boulders. It looked dangerous.

Another few days of travel brought them and the river to the valley floor. The valley stretched out in front of them, widening as it went. The vegetation was much greener here, and many birds sang in the trees. Deer moved in and out of the shadows. Boy noticed a raccoon's paw print in the mud by the river. It looked almost like a tiny human hand with five long fingers.

He also noticed coyote prints that looked like a wolf print, but smaller. He did not see any sign of a wolf pack in this area.

Wind in the Grass was tiring, but moved with determination. He explained the people went many miles more south to spend the winter on the edge of the plains. Wood was readily available, as were buffalo. The clan may have started back north to one of their many summer hunting grounds. Wind and Spear would have to keep moving until they met up with the people or at least crossed their trail.

They camped in the valley and decided to stay two days to rest. They had eaten most of their dried meat, but rabbits and fish had fed them along the way as well. Wind told Spear that if they ran out of meat before they found his people, they would hunt a young deer with their bows and would dry the meat before going further. For now they would continue to travel trying to find his people.

The next day they walked along the trail through a grove of quaking aspen trees. Spear walked silently behind the old scout, paying more attention to the tracks along the trail than to his surroundings. Wind suddenly stopped and abruptly turned around directly in front of Spear. He spoke loudly again as if he was talking to more than just his traveling companion.

Looking into the boy's eyes, Wind said, "Perhaps a scout is not as good as he thinks!"

Spear was puzzled by this statement. He hadn't claimed to be a scout. What brought on this apparent insult anyway?

Spear was just about to protest, when another booming voice said in Wind's language: "Perhaps a scout just wanted to greet an old friend!"

With that, a man stepped out of the bushes so close to Spear that it made him jump to the side of the trail.

The man barely noticed Spear as he grabbed Wind's good arm in a greeting.

Smiling, he said, "Looks as though my friend has weathered a rough winter!" indicating the wounded leg and fresh wounds to his arm.

"Not as tough as it might have been!" was Wind's answer. "Thanks to my new friend, Wolf Who Kills with a Spear!" and waved his hand in the boy's direction.

Turning to Spear, Wind said, "This is Eagle Flying, another scout of my clan!"

"We thought you were dead," Eagle Flying said. "We looked for you when you did not return as you had promised. Hunting Weasel found where three men had been killed and mostly eaten by a large bear. One was not you, but the others had little left to determine who they might have been. Your trail had led to the battle site, but not away from it!"

"This is true," said Wind. "But as you can see, I have survived."

"And this young warrior, with a name bigger than he is, helped you do that?" Eagle Flying was shaking his head in disbelief. "I am sure it is a good story, and a long one if told correctly! I look forward to hearing it in council. I will report to the elders and tell of your return. You will find the encampment at the bottom of the drop at the end of this valley next to the river. The hunters are gathering deer meat and the women are making buckskin."

With that, Eagle Flying turned and melted back into the brush.

Wind turned to Spear and said, "By tomorrow night, we will sit in a council of my people and tell them your story! We will tell them of Mother Wolf, and of her wolf pup and her human pup and how they lived together and hunted together, and saved an old scout's life. We will be honored with drumming, singing, and dancing! The women will bring us their best prepared foods, the hunters and warriors will scoff and call us liars, but all the time they will be jealous of our adventures. Now let us make camp just up the trail there by the pool in the river. We will bathe and wash our hair, clean our buckskins, and walk into camp tomorrow with our heads high and showing the true people, we are proud, brave, and have a story to tell!"

Wolf Who Kills with a Spear was grinning at the thought of the celebration, though he was uncertain about meeting that many people all at once. Turning to look back up the trail, he thought of all that had happened, how far he had come. He thought of how he could have died many times, but he had survived. He thought about all he had learned and the family he had made. He missed the woman who had taken care of him as a child, he missed his wolf mother, he missed his wolf brother. But now he had Wind in the Grass, his teacher, his mentor.

"Hey!" hollered Wind as he plunged naked into the river. "How am I to introduce a young warrior to the people when he stinks like an old sow bear?

Spear pulled off his shirt, "I will be as clean as you, old man!" he hollered, "but I will be much better looking!"

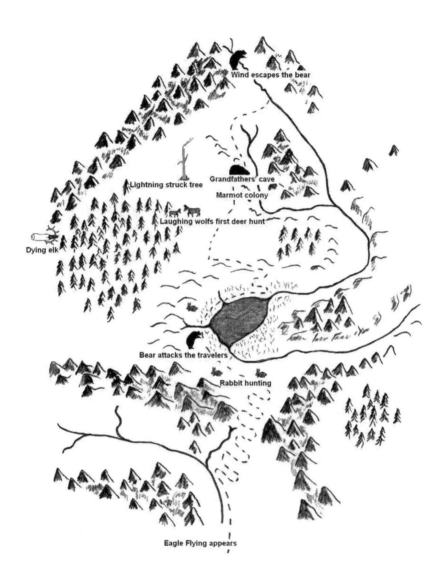

Wind escapes the bear

Lightning struck tree

Grandfathers' cave

Marmot colony

Laughing wolfs first deer hunt

Dying elk

Bear attacks the travelers

Rabbit hunting

Eagle Flying appears

ABOUT THE AUTHOR

I am by no means an expert in primitive or survival skills. I consider myself a student on a lifelong educational journey. I have many friends who are more experienced in primitive skills than I am, but I have hunted with a bow and arrow for 45 years, big game for 36 of those years. My experience in hunting and archery has always lead me to want to know more about the primitive peoples who made their living with the tools they made themselves. My friends have taught me much, and I have read books by authors who have inspired me to learn even more. I thank them all for their contribution to my life experiences. I hope this book will encourage others to look into the study of primitive skills.

I grew up on a ranch in eastern Oregon. My family has always been animal oriented. We had the requisite horses, cows, and dogs that a ranch is usually home to, but we also had some uncommon pets. One I recall fondly was a pet badger named Mac that came from a plowed-up burrow in a relative's field. I was quite young but still remember Mac around the house. As he grew, we had to move him out to a cattle pasture to keep him from greeting startled guests.

Dad once got a call from a neighbor who asked, "Are you the guy with the pet badger?"

"Yes," Dad answered.

"I was out irrigating when a badger came running at me. I ran for the open door of my truck, but the badger beat me there and is now sitting in the cab. Can you come get him?"

This was years before cell phones, so I can only imagine the farmer walked all the way back to his house to make the call. Dad went and claimed Mac, and we are left with this story that I love to tell. We also had a pet Kestrel hawk, Frightful, named after the red tailed hawk in the movie "My Side of the Mountain." Dad brought this pet home as a white ball of fluff from an old, abandoned house he was tearing down. We fed Frightful raw hamburger until it took flight. It was quite friendly, although the shirtless high school boys my granddad hired to stack hay were not thrilled when it landed on their bare shoulders without warning. Frightful had an affinity for landing on Mom's head and stomping around in her hair.

From a young age I was fascinated with primitive peoples and life ways. Finding stone points in my grandfather's field, I marveled at the craftsmanship and wondered just how they had been made. At age eight I took up bow hunting. My parents gave me a fiberglass longbow. My grandfather offered to pay me for ground squirrel tails if I shot squirrels out of his hay field. The bounty was a penny for a squirrel tail shot with a .22 caliber rifle, a nickel for one taken with my BB gun, or a dime for one taken with my bow. I got a lot of practice shooting my bow, if not a pocket full of change. I continued with my interest in all things archery, learning to make my own arrows from commercial materials.

My dad kept a well-equipped woodshop. He taught me and my two brothers how to work wood from a young age. By high school, I was a bit more advanced than most students in woodshop class. I was allowed to attempt larger projects like building a kayak. It did float for a bit, but it was really just a wildly uneducated attempt at boat making. It left in me a yearning to build a working kayak, but I wanted it to be more like the ones I read about made by the native peoples of Alaska. I learned leather tooling from a high school friend in 1976. A lifelong creative activity, leather working piqued my interest for tanning my own hides and sewing my own buckskin clothing.

I worked the summer of 1976 at a Youth Conservation Corps Camp on the Malheur National Wildlife Refuge in Southeast Oregon. While riding the bus on my way there, I saw a man in a loin cloth poling a handmade reed boat. The bus driver told me his name and I committed it to memory. I vowed I would meet that man one day. It would be 20 years later before I finally did. The library at the refuge had a book, *Outdoor Survival Skills* by Larry Dean Olsen. I told my mother about it in a letter home. She brought me a new copy, the one I still have today, when she picked me up at the end of the summer. Using this book, I tried making my first bow, a choke cherry survival bow that was too weak and short for my arms. I hung it on my wall as a decoration.

As life grew me into a young adult, I followed other interests. In 1980 I became a father, busy raising my children. My outdoors activities gave way to making a living. I moved to the city and concentrated on providing for my family. I tried to get out hunting every year. I joined different archery clubs over the years to keep me shooting my bows. As a member of the Sylvan Archers of Portland, I started my kids shooting, each beginning at age two. They first learned to shoot using the choke cherry bow I had made in high school. Their arrows were my old broken shafts that I whittled to a point so they would stick in a target bale.

I was lucky enough to be involved with the beginning of the Traditional Archers of Oregon. I drew the logo for the club as it was forming. Later a local traditional archery club formed and I won the logo drawing contest for Black Rose Traditional Archers of Tigard, Oregon.

It was in 1995 as a member of this Black Rose Archery Club that I was finally introduced to flint knapping. Though I had read about knapping, I had not witnessed anybody doing it. The brief demonstration occurred at one of our monthly meetings. The eager soul had just knapped for the first time the week before, but he gave me enough visual information to get started. I found an antler tine and broke up an obsidian cobble I had brought back on one of my hunting trips. It was a rough imitation of a point, very crude and not straight or sharp at all. I keep it to see how far I have come.

In 1996 I moved back to my parents' ranch. I joined the Eagle Cap Traditional Archers in La Grande, Oregon. As luck would have it, I ended up drawing a logo for them as well.

It was at this time I met one of my best friends and fellow primitive skills practitioner, Bradley Phillips. We keep each other practicing and learning. Bradley introduced me to the late Rex Watson. Rex was a master flint knapper, archaeologist, and artist. He taught us to percussion flake and improved both of our knapping abilities tenfold. Bradley was the person who finally introduced me to the man on the reed boat I'd seen so many years before. Jim Riggs has spent most of his life learning and teaching primitive skills. He is one of the best knappers I have ever seen work, though I am now acquainted with many of his friends and students who are incredible knappers in their own right. Bradley introduced me to Jim Riggs at his annual Glass Buttes Knap-in. The knap-in occurs in March in southeast Oregon, only about fifty miles from where I had seen Jim so many years before. I have met many a good friend at this knap-in even though I have not attended every year.

My family have always been hunters. I took my first deer at age ten with a rifle. I took my first bow-killed deer at age seventeen using a compound bow. It was a two by two point mule deer buck I shot at four yards. I took many deer and an Alaskan moose with my compound bows. At age twenty-three, I graduated from my compound to a custom made wood and fiberglass long bow made by John Strunk. I took many deer, elk, and two bears with that bow. John became a renowned primitive bowyer, and years later he sold me a yew stave backed with bamboo with which I made my first homemade hunting weight bow. I progressed to making all my own homemade equipment.

Sometime in my thirties, I took up wood carving, making canes, bowls, and walking sticks. I eventually carved the stalk of a black powder rifle I built from a kit.

I have always had a love of music. I was a drummer in high school band, so my primitive skills interests lead me to make a rawhide drum with a steam-bent frame of quaking aspen. It needs a fire to warm it up to get to its best voice. I bought a guitar and taught myself to play. I mostly play for friends, but I have enjoyed playing around the campfire at primitive gatherings.

Sometime in my forties I was introduced to Dave Clemmons of Richland, Oregon. He was selling Native American style flutes at a festival in my home town. I bought a couple of flutes and he showed me the fingering. I taught myself to play and kept returning to Dave for more flutes. He suggested he could teach me to make them myself and so I jumped at the chance. Combined with my wood-carving abilities, my elderberry wood flutes are pretty and functional. I aspire to reach Dave's ability to make concert-level flutes. He is indeed a master. I will keep practicing this skill until I get it right.

In 2009 I read about a skin-on-frame kayak class being taught by Kiliii Yu of Sea Wolf Kayaks. I could make an ocean-going kayak called the "Stellar" which was Kiliii's design, but based on techniques used by his ancestors in Arctic Russia. Instead of a walrus hide for a cover, we would use modern materials. The only metal in the boat would be brass tacks in the combing. The rest of the boat would be pegged or tied together. I had to do it!

In 2013 I had the privilege of making another boat with Kiliii Yu, and Patrick Farneman, another of my primitive skills friends. The "Inlander" was designed by Patrick and is similar to the Stellar, but shorter and more maneuverable for small rivers.

Bradley Phillips and his family encouraged me to come with them in 2010 to my first general primitive skills gathering called Echoes In Time. I took a class on primitive pottery, learning to make and fire my first pot in a campfire. I made my first pack basket out of willow. I was privileged to be able to offer suggestions to people just learning skills I had been practicing for some time. I also ran into friends from The Glass Buttes knap-in and made new friends as well. I returned the following year as a student again, but the third year I went as a teacher's assistant to Aaron Webster, the bow making instructor. Through online pictures of a private flint knapping class I gave to some fellow outdoor enthusiasts, I was invited to do a flint knapping demonstration and subsequent classes for the Oregon Trail Interpretive Center in Baker City. I was also invited to teach knapping at a gathering in Northeastern Washington called Between the Rivers.

Bow hunting has been my lifelong interest and the stimulus to expanding my knowledge in primitive skills. With each reduction of the capabilities of my hunting equipment, I learned to get closer to the animal I was hunting. In 2009, I took a five-point bull elk with a homemade bow of Ipe and black bamboo, using arrows of wild rose tipped with my own knapped obsidian points. It was a triumph for me personally and the culmination of the primitive skills I have learned to this point.

SUGGESTED READINGS

Brown, Tom Jr. *Tom Brown Jr.'s Field Guide Series.* New York: Berkley Books.

Elbroch, Mark. *Mammal Tracks & Sign: A Guide to North American Species.* Mechanicsburg, Penn.: Stackpole Books, 2003.

Hamm, Jim. *Bows and Arrows of the Native Americans: A Complete Step-by-Step Guide to Wooden Bows, Sinew-Backed Bows, Composite Bows, Strings, Arrows and Quivers.* Guilford, Conn.: Lyons Press, 2007.

Hamm, Jim, ed. *The Traditional Bowyers Bible* series. Guilford, Conn.: Lyons Press, 2000.

McPherson, John and McPherson, Geri. *Primitive Wilderness Living & Survival Skills: Naked into the Wilderness.* Randolph, Kan.: Prairie Wolf Publishing, 1993. Updated version: *Updated Guide to Wilderness Living: Surviving with Nothing but your Bare Hands and What You Find in the Woods.* Berkeley, Calif.: Ulysses Press, 2008.

Olsen, Larry Dean. *Outdoor Survival Skills, 6th ed.* Chicago: Chicago Review Press, 1997.

Peterson Field Guide Series (Birds, Mammals, Reptiles, Trees, Medicinal Plants, more). New York: Houghton Mifflin Harcourt.

Riggs, Jim. *Blue Mountain Buckskin: A Working Manual for Dry-Scrape Brain-Tan,* 2d ed. Ashland, Ore.: Backcountry Publishing, 2004.

Tilford, Gregory L. *Edible and Medicinal Plants of the West.* Missoula, Mont.: Mountain Press Publishing Company, 1997.

Young, Jon. Advanced Bird Language: Reading Concentric Rings of Nature, 8 CDs. Duvall, Wash.: Wilderness Awareness School. http://wildernessawareness.org/

SAMPLING OF

PRIMITIVE SKILLS GATHERINGS

IN THE WESTERN UNITED STATES

Winter Count:

Location: Near Phoenix, Arizona

When: Mid-February

Website: http://www.backtracks.net/wintercount.html

Buckeye Gathering: Ancestral Arts and Technology

Location: Lake Concow Campground, Forestville, California

When: Late April to early May

Website: http://buckeyegathering.net/

Between The Rivers Gathering

Location: Valley, Washington (40 miles north of Spokane)

When: Late May

Website: http://www.betweentheriversgathering.com/

Echoes in Time: Workshops in Early Living Skills

Location: Champoeg State Park, St. Paul, Oregon (west of I-5 between Portland and Salem)

When: Late July

Website: http://www.echoes-in-time.com/

Rabbit Stick

Location: Rexburg, Idaho

When: Mid-September

Website: http://www.backtracks.net/rabbitstick.html

GLOSSARY

Bow drill: A mechanism where a small bow with its bowstring wrapped around a drill shaft is used to spin the shaft in both directions while the shaft is pressured from the upper end.

Brain tanning: The art of using an animal's brain, with smoke, to permanently soften its hide for material use.

Full draw: Pulling a bow's string back to the full extent the shooter's arms will allow.

Flint knapping: The art of breaking rock in a manner that produces a usable sharp blade.

Knock: The notched end of an arrow that is fitted to the string of a bow.

Pressure flaking: Breaking flakes off of a stone core in a specific direction using arm/ hand pressure through a tool.

Percussion flaking: Breaking flakes off of a stone core in a specific direction using a hammering or percussion force through a tool.

Spalled flake: A large stone flake broken off a stone core by percussion flaking.

Stave: The cut piece of a tree or tree limb to be made into a bow.

Tillered bow: A bow in the process of being built, after it has been shaped enough to bend without breaking.

Made in the USA
San Bernardino, CA
21 September 2014